"I guess this is goodbye."

"Yes." Brianna McKaslin shrugged out of his jacket with graceful movements and handed him the garment. "Here's hoping we both have better luck on our next blind dates."

"Sure." It was all he could think to say. Max Decker, the man who had a comeback for any occasion, stood speechless as she cast him one last look. Her gaze met his like a bolt of electricity and it jarred his system, leaving him rooted to the spot.

Amazing. He watched as she glided away, unaware of what she'd done to him with one single glance. His heart had stopped beating. The blood was stalled in his veins. He struggled for air as she walked away with her gentle, easy gait, her sleek, straight hair brushing her shoulder blades with each step.

Why was he captivated? Was it sympathy for her or something more?

JILLIAN HART

grew up on her family's homestead, where she raised cattle, rode horses and scribbled stories in her spare time. After earning her English degree from Whitman College, she worked in travel and advertising before selling her first novel. When Jillian isn't working on her next story, she can be found puttering in her rose garden, curled up with a good book and spending quiet evenings at home with her family.

Blind-Date Bride
Jillian Hart

Steeple
Hill®

Published by Steeple Hill Books™

STEEPLE HILL BOOKS

**Steeple
Hill**®

ISBN-13: 978-0-373-81405-3
ISBN-10:   0-373-81405-4

Recycling programs
for this product may
not exist in your area.

BLIND-DATE BRIDE

www.SteepleHill.com

Printed in U.S.A.

There is no fear in love;
but perfect love casts out fear.

—1 *John* 4:18

Chapter One

It happened again. Another blind date gone wrong. No, worse than wrong. It hadn't even started.

Brianna McKaslin let the edge of her sleeve slip into place, hiding the watch that said her supposed-to-be-perfect match was thirty-five minutes late. And counting.

Thirty-five minutes? Too late to be caught in traffic, not in this part of town. Bozeman, Montana, wasn't that big of a place, so anything over half an hour meant she'd been officially dumped.

Guess what, Bree? He's not coming. She leaned back in the chair and stretched her feet out under the table. Time to de-stress. This was, what, the third first date in a row to leave her solo in a restaurant? What was with men, anyway? Were they that commitment shy? Or was it something about her?

She took a sip of cooling tea but the soothing heat and sweetness didn't comfort her. Not one bit. She caught a glimpse of herself in the mirrored display case. An average-looking girl stared back at her. She might not possess a stunning fashion sense and/or spend hours at a mirror trying to enhance her appearance with a mascara wand and a curling iron. But all in all, she wasn't so unattractive that she'd sent three poor men running to escape her, was she? Or did men come equipped with X-ray vision that could see past her plain straight hair and the average girl she was to the deeper flaws inside?

She let out a frustrated sigh. She had a lot of pent-up frustration at the male gender in general. Whatever committed, stable, loving men were out there, they seemed to avoid her like an I.R.S. audit.

She wanted to be married. Settled. Secure. Loved. Was that too much to ask?

Maybe. She straightened up in the chair, brushed the too-long bangs out of her eyes and gave the dregs in her teacup a final sip.

I'm not destined to be alone, right, Lord? No answer came blazing down from above. She sure hoped it wasn't true. Alone was a painful place to be. She set the cup in its saucer with a clink and looked around at the other customers. She studied the few couples, obviously out on dates, seated on opposite sides of the tables, holding hands, leaning over their desserts and specialty coffees, chatting, their gazes locked together.

Could she help it if a sigh of longing escaped? Those couples had been able to find each other. And here she sat alone, the vision of romantic doom.

Maybe chocolate would help. A girl might not be able to count on a man, but a good piece of chocolate never let her down. She twisted in her seat to get a good look at the bakery's display case packed with comforting sweets. It all looked so good. Maybe she would spring for a slice of triple-chocolate cake with fudge frosting. It was one of her favorites, and she had decorated it this morning. This was also her place of employment, where she was working her way very slowly through college.

A blur of movement flashed in the display's mirror. The blur became a guy lumbering up to the front door. Could it be her mystery date? Did she dare hope? She whipped around to get a better look. There was a lanky, rather shorter guy around her age—twenty-twoish—with dark shades and slicked-back hair. In black leather jacket and tight pants, he wouldn't look out of place in a twentysomething motorcycle gang or a gang of any kind.

Definitely *not* her kind of guy. He was *not* the man she'd come to meet, right?

She ought to go order that wedge of cake, but curiosity kept her watching. The gang guy planted his heavy biker's boots and scanned the length of the bakery's dozen bistro tables, wearing the reserved look of a man about to meet with his tax accountant.

She gulped; she couldn't help it. What if he was looking for her? What if he *was* Billy, the man her half sister swore was The One? No, no, no, no. She clutched the wide ceramic mug in panic.

His gaze locked on hers through the glass for one brief, mind-numbing moment. The nose ring dangling from his left nostril twinkled in the late evening sunlight. Not that she was interested, but she couldn't help wondering. How does one go about kissing a man with a nose ring? Wouldn't it get in the way? For a woman with marriage on her mind, this was an important question.

His black eyes flashed wide in what had to be terror. He jerked his head away, plunged his fists in his jacket pockets and hurried away as fast as his boots could carry him.

Disaster avoided. Whew. And if that *was* Billy,

then what had Colbie been thinking? Her sister had described him as a nice Christian man. That's what Brianna wanted—and one with a good job and an excellent credit history, of course.

Mr. Nose Ring was long gone, but he had been a good reminder. The next time she agreed to a blind date, she would have to be sure and add "no body piercings" to her long list.

Her watch said six forty-four.

"I notice you're still sitting alone." Brandilyn, her twin, set a fresh pot of hot water with a new tea bag on the table and cleared away the empty one. "He didn't show up?"

Brianna shook her head and reached for the sugar. "He got a good look at me through the window and kept on going. Next time I'm going to sit in the back against the wall, so the dude has to come in and reject me face-to-face."

"What kind of guy in his right mind would reject you? Goodness." A great sister, that's what Brandilyn was, and Brianna cherished her more than anything on this earth. The chime above the door jingled. "Wow. Take a look over your shoulder at the hunk just walking in. Maybe he's Billy."

"I see him." No nose ring. And he looked *good*. Too good. He was the right kind of tall—

not gargantuan but tall enough to look up to with a sigh. His wide shoulders and his granite profile were a dream. He was Mr. Perfect. He could have stepped off the front of a magazine, all rugged good looks and presence. He exuded masculine appeal from twenty feet away as he ran a well-shaped hand through his dark hair.

What would it be like to feel his broad palm against hers? For a nanosecond, she let herself dream that he had come to meet her. That she was the woman he had been waiting for, the one who would capture all of his heart.

Then she decided to get real. "There's no way he's Billy. My track record isn't that good."

"But prayer is, and I've been praying hard for you, Bree. There's no reason why you can't find a great guy and be happy ever after."

If there were any great guys out there. *If* she didn't wind up with their mother's pattern with men. Brianna bit her tongue. Hadn't she decided to banish those difficult thoughts? She was trying to think positively. After all, she and her sister had something their mother didn't— faith and prayer.

Brandilyn had a point. There had to be happiness out there for them somewhere. "Isn't that God's promise? That He has happiness in store for us, a good future and hope?"

"You're right," Bree told her sister, knowing Brandilyn needed to hear it more than she did. "I'm sure God has something very special in mind for both of us."

Maybe the kind of close family life that had always eluded them. It was hard when a girl had to raise herself. Bree was infinitely grateful for her twin. They had each other, and that had helped cushion some of life's harder moments. She had to believe that God would one day lead both of them to good husbands and the family life they both hungered for.

If this dating thing would ever work out, that is. Bree rolled her eyes. Back to the man at the front. She twisted in her chair to get a better look at him. He had stalked up to the counter, waiting his turn in line. As he studied the menu high on the wall behind the counter, his head was tilted back just enough that she could see a cowlick at the crown. He had thick hair that was nicely kept and brushed at the collar of his jacket. He was too gorgeous. No way was he here on a blind date.

"Why don't I ever get set up with a guy like that?" Brandilyn lamented. "Wait, I already know the answer."

"A man like that doesn't need to be set up." And a girl like her did.

"Waitress?" someone in the back called out.

"Gotta go." Brandi gave a "too bad" look before she slipped off to check on the customer.

Yes, it was totally too bad. Brianna went back to reading her inspirational romance. Forget Mr. Perfect and concentrate on fictional happy-ever-afters. Those happened much more frequently. She wasn't even sure if girls like her—who had grown up poor with a childhood full of chaos—ever had the chance for happy endings. All she had was blind faith. And—she smiled up as her twin walked by and left a plate on the table's edge—chocolate cake.

Excellent. She nudged the plate closer, and a pair of hiking books, scuffed and masculine, came into her field of sight. A strange prickle skidded down her spine, like a warning of doom or a sign of good things to come—she didn't know which.

"Excuse me. You wouldn't happen to be Alice, would you?"

It was the handsome guy. His voice rumbled deep as an evening storm. With one look into his captivating blue eyes, the power of speech abandoned her. Fabulous. Since she wasn't Alice, she managed a slight shake of her head.

"No? That's too bad. All I know is that she's supposed to be blond." He shrugged a wide shoulder beneath the dark shirt he wore. "Sorry to bother you."

"No problem." Thank the heavens her power of speech returned. "I was waiting for someone, too, but I think he spied me through the window and ran away in terror. I must have scared him off, the poor guy."

"Seems like a dim bulb to me."

What a nice guy to say that and what a nice grin he had, softening the craggy ruggedness of his features. Wow. "Trust me, it's for the best. He had a nose ring and a gang attitude. There's no way it would have worked out past the introduction."

"I've had that happen before." The left corner of his mouth hooked in a small grin. "That's why I've given up on blind dates. No, don't say it. This is an exception. One of my best buddies promised I wouldn't regret this. I hope Alice wasn't that woman with an orange Mohawk I passed by in the parking lot."

"Maybe she was looking for the Nose Ring guy."

"I guess there's someone for everyone." When he smiled wider, dimples cut into his lean cheeks.

Double wow. The din from the surrounding tables faded away into silence. For one instant, just for one little millisecond, nothing existed but the tall, incredible-looking man towering over her. He could have walked off the pages of her romance novel. If perfection were a ten, this man was a twenty.

Yep, definitely out of her league. Too bad. She had to get real. She was turning over a new leaf with her realistic but positive thoughts and finding stability in her life—or least she was trying to. That was the plan. The right man was out there somewhere. She had faith, right? A movement outside caught her attention. "There's someone coming up to the door now. Maybe Alice?"

"She's not blond. I know it's none of my business, but why are you waiting for a blind date? You don't need to be set up. Guys must flock around you."

"Yes, of course." She gestured to the space around her table where no men flocked. "I'm surprised you could approach the table with all the guys crowded around me."

"Beautiful *and* a sense of humor." Although he was a tough-looking guy, his dimples deepened. Triple wow. "I'm Max."

"I'm Brianna. It's nice to meet you. Now tell me why *you* are on a blind date."

"I've gotten cynical and I can't keep a girlfriend." His smile belied his words, and a hint of sadness cut into his face. There was a story there, one she suddenly wanted to hear. Had he been unlucky in love, the way she had? Had he been hurt or deceived? Or did relationships simply never work out for him? "I had a tough break up a long while back and some of my work buddies think I should get out more."

"That's the argument my sister Colbie used to get me here."

"Have you ever noticed that the people who set you up on a blind date actually never go out on them?"

"Yes. They don't have to go through the torture of trying to make conversation with a complete stranger, or finding out again that no, it's just another date failure."

"I've had a lot of date failures." He straightened his shoulders a bit as he said that.

It was hard to imagine Max had had failures. He seemed perfect, exactly what she wanted. A real man who would treat her right. Who would protect her and make her feel completely safe. After all she had been through over the past year and beyond, that thought felt as welcome as paradise.

"I don't believe it." She shook her head. "You are not the kind of guy to have date failures."

"I hate to break it to you, but everyone has a bad dating tale to tell." He curled his hand over the back of the chair and gave it a tug. "Do you mind?"

"Please, sit and tell me what could possibly have been more disastrous than being rejected on sight by three dates in a row."

"There was the time I met my work buddy's wife's best friend." He eased into the chair with an athlete's confidence. His dark shock of hair tumbled over his brow, making him look rakish. "We all went to the county fair together."

"Sounds like fun unless you are the type of guy who doesn't like livestock and fair burgers."

"You say that like you think I'm not."

"It did occur to me. You might rather go to a ball game or, wait, a car racetrack."

"I don't approve of speeding." He gave her his best grin. He didn't know why he was talking to this woman. Okay, maybe he did. She was adorable with big violet-blue eyes and a sweetheart's smile. But that wasn't why he had sat down at her table. There was something more to her, something he couldn't place his finger on. "The problem was that every time she talked, she mentioned weddings."

"I get it. You're a guy who doesn't believe in commitment, right?"

"Hey, wait a minute. You're leaping fast to all the wrong conclusions about me."

"Am I?" She folded a stray strand of light

blond hair behind her ear. She had an elegant way of moving, and he liked the combination of casual elegance and nice, hometown girl. Not that he believed in appearances, not with his job. As a detective, he had learned the hard way that no one is what they seemed to be. But he liked thinking it was possible to find a truly sweet woman who was as nice and as guileless as her smile. Not that he believed it.

"I'm one of the good guys. Or I try to be." That was the truth. He tried as hard as he knew how to walk that narrow straight line. Not easy in this world. "Anyway, I'm with my buddy, his wife and her best friend and I'm on my best behavior. Trying to be suave, you know, impress the lady."

"Did it work?"

"Nope. Talking and walking was beyond me that day. I ran into a garbage can, a utility pole, miscalculated in the crowd and stepped on the back of my date's shoe, pitching her forward into the sheep tent."

"Was she okay? How did the sheep handle it?"

"I didn't know something harmless and innocent could ram a gate so hard. I got her out of the way just in time, but she had sprained her ankle and cut her hand." He shook his head. Why was he admitting this? "See, we all have bad dates. But I recovered."

"Oh, so she forgave you and went on a second date?"

"No, no second dates yet, but I keep hoping."

"You told me a story to make me feel better, didn't you? That didn't really happen. I can't see it." Her gaze raked over him, as if she were sizing him up and making her own judgments on his character. "I'm sure women fall at your feet."

"Only unless I trip them accidentally." He rolled his eyes. "To be fair, I haven't done that before or since, but I use it as a yardstick to measure my long string of date failures against. No matter how bad things are, it's nowhere near as bad as that date turned out."

"Turned out? You mean there's more to the story?" She leaned forward expectantly.

Call him a fool, but he couldn't resist making her smile a little more. She was striking, not just beautiful, and totally wholesome. Maybe it was the soft pink sweater she wore. With her blond hair and blue eyes, she looked like a storybook princess. Not that he was searching for that, but a guy liked to believe somewhere there was goodness in the world, that someone somewhere was good through and through.

He felt like a fool, but he went on with the tale. What was his dignity next to seeing the hint of sadness gone from her face? "The final straw was when I slipped down two bleacher steps when we stopped to watch the roping competition. She suddenly remembered an appointment and ran in terror."

"From the looks of you, I never would have suspected you were such a scary dude."

"Frightening." He felt comfortable with her, right off. That was something he never felt around a woman. Maybe because he wasn't actually dating her.

Then it hit him. He knew what had been bugging him about her. He'd seen her before. The snapshot flashed into his head. He saw the image of her face but without the smile and the warmth of laughter in her eyes. Her hair had been shorter then, hanging straight and lifeless, thoroughly wet from the rain. Brianna had been a crime victim. He'd worked on part of the case last summer.

The door opened on a gust of cool air and the chime above jangled, cutting through his thoughts. He felt a tingle on the back of his neck, as if someone was looking him over. In walked a tall, well-tailored woman. Her thin leather briefcase was tucked beneath her arm and her designer suit skirt swirled tastefully around her slender calves.

She crooked one penciled eyebrow in silent question.

If this lady was Alice, then Dobbs had gotten it wrong again. Best go deal with this. "I guess I had better go see if that's my date."

"Sure, you don't want someone like that getting away."

With a wink, he rose from the chair, taking his regrets with him. Only when he really knew to look for them did he see the shadows in Brianna's eyes.

Her smile was genuine as she gave him a finger wave. "She's pretty. She could be The One. Here's hoping."

Hope? He would need more than that. He was going to need Providence to see him through a piece of cake and a cup of decaf with the woman who *should* be right for any man, but he knew in his gut if that woman was Alice, she couldn't be more wrong for him.

He gave Brianna a nod for goodbye and let his feet take him toward the woman waiting for him at the counter.

Chapter Two

"I'm sorry," Brandilyn whispered as she paused on her way by, carrying a loaded tray. "I had hoped he was Billy."

"Tall, dark and rugged isn't my type." Brianna put down her book, gathered up her empty plate, fork and tea things. She may as well clear her own table and save her twin a little bit of work.

Out of the corner of her eye, she caught sight of Max. Apparently the woman wasn't Alice, but he had ordered a beverage anyway and had retreated to the only empty table in the bakery, which happened to be in the far corner. Totally her luck. He had pulled a book out of his jacket pocket—not that she was watching or anything, but she couldn't help noticing.

And so did the blond woman who was not Alice. She sat at a table alone, too, but across the aisle from Max. Not Alice kept making eye contact and smiling at him.

Of course, Bree didn't blame the woman one bit. They made a handsome couple. His dark good looks and her golden ones. The woman was perfect. She had a delicate beauty and impeccable accessorizing skills. Her shoes, hose and purse matched her designer-label outfit. She was probably exactly what Max went for. Good for her.

"I thought that was exactly the kind of man you were looking for." Her sister wasn't easily fooled.

"Maybe I should leave the looking to God."

"You're right, but it's hard to wait."

Waiting was the story of her life. She said goodbye to her twin and slipped into her coat. It was March and while the day had been sunny, the dusk was approaching and with it the chilly night. She slung her pink plaid backpack over one shoulder, bussed her dishes and headed out. She kept her eyes on the door and then on the parking lot. She didn't want to catch accidental sight of Max.

Ever since the robbery last summer when she'd very nearly lost her life, she'd had a hard time feeling anything. Sometimes it was as if her heart had simply turned off. Other times, she felt too much, like now.

Some days it was best to be numb. Her shoes tapped against the concrete sidewalk and the wind pressed like ice against her face and bare hands. She hated walking alone. It didn't matter that the parking lot was well lit or in perfect view of the bakery. She fished her keys out of her coat pocket and held them ready. She tucked the mini can of pepper spray attached to her key ring in her palm. Probably totally unnecessary in this small city, but she felt better, stronger, as she tapped through the fading daylight.

See, she was safe. The deep-seated dread squeezing her was from the posttraumatic stress, that was all. She was fine. She stepped off the curb, and a car door slammed. The sound rattled through her like a gunshot. A guy emerged from between the cars wearing a Montana State University sweatshirt and a backpack. He walked toward her.

She swallowed hard. She was fine. Nothing was going to happen. Good thing the sun hadn't gone all the way down. She was in full view of the bakery's wide picture windows where all sorts of people could see her. She trembled, unable to shake the fear that had taken root in her bones.

Nothing bad is going to happen, she reminded herself, fighting for calm. The counselor had warned this would simply take time. There was nothing wrong with being afraid. She needed only to have the courage to face it. One day, the fear and the residual trauma would be gone.

That was the plan, anyway. She cut between a pickup and an SUV and froze at the empty parking spot. Where had her car gone? This was the correct place, right? She turned around, scanning the small lot, already knowing the truth in her gut. Someone had stolen her car. She shivered deep inside.

It's just a car, she told herself. No one was hurt. She was safe.

Then why was adrenaline crackling through her? She trembled, fighting the pull of fear. The past was right there—the trauma she hadn't completely dealt with—and she wasn't going to let it pull her down. There wasn't a gunman holding a semi-automatic to her temple. There wasn't anyone critically hurt and crying out with terror echoing in her memory. She gave thanks that this wasn't the same at all.

"Do you always hang out in parking lots?" a familiar baritone rumbled behind her.

She whipped around, relieved to see Max standing in the golden slant of light. He appeared trustworthy standing there with his hands on his hips, emphasizing the dependable line of his shoulders. He looked like someone she could trust. "I left my car here, but I guess it took off without me."

"You mean someone stole it?"

"Incredibly. I can't imagine anyone would want it." While she was grateful for a working car, the fourteen-year-old Chevy had seen better days. "I know I locked it. I'm compulsive about that sort of thing."

"Locks won't stop a car thief." Max pulled his cell phone out of his jacket pocket and flipped it open. "I'll get a uniform over here to take your statement."

"The police?" Brianna gulped in air, fighting to keep calm. They would come with their flashing lights and their badges. It would remind her of that night. She shivered.

This wasn't the same thing, she told herself. This was a case of a missing car, nothing more. It didn't mean her foundation had to be rattled. It didn't mean she had to be catapulted back in time.

"Brianna?" Max's voice came as if from far away. "Hey, are you all right?"

"F-fine." Any minute now he was probably going to think she was loony tunes. A real nut bar. Shame crashed through her like a cold wave. "I'm just a little shocked."

"No, this is more than shock." His palm

curved over her shoulder, his grip strong and comforting. "You're shaking. Come with me."

His grip remained, holding her emotions steady as she put one foot in front of the other. She thought of all the ways this evening was different from the one her mind would not let go of. She carefully catalogued them. It was nearly sunset now and bold colors stained the sky. She was outside, breathing in the crisp evening breeze instead of the heated, food-scented air in the kitchen of the restaurant where she'd been working last summer. So much was different right now, but that didn't seem to matter to her brain.

The images came anyway, flashes of chaos and agony and panic. She blinked away the pictures of violence and blood and concentrated on the pavement solid beneath her shoes, the traffic whipping by on the nearby street and the gleaming neon sign from the dry cleaner in the next building over.

Tonight was not the same, she thought as Max guided her down the row of parked cars. Her foundation hadn't crumbled. She didn't have to flash back to that terror-filled kitchen. The ground felt more solid beneath her feet with every step she took. Her shoes tapped on the blacktop and she concentrated on the straight broad line of Max's back and his reassuring presence a half a step ahead of her. The past faded, she felt whole again. Thank heavens there had been no full-fledged panic attack.

Cool wind fanned her hot face. She waited while he opened the passenger door to a shiny white truck. It felt nice standing beside him. He towered over her, and for all his strength he felt kind, not intimidating. His grip on her elbow was firm and caring all at once as he helped her onto the comfy leather seat.

"Better?" He shrugged out of his coat.

She nodded. "And here you're thinking, she looked so normal sitting in the bakery."

"What you're going through *is* normal." He leaned close, bringing with him the scents of coffee and cake and the masculine pine scent of his aftershave. His breath was warm against her neck as he draped his coat over her shoulders.

The garment's weight hugged her and its heat soothed. Bree studied the man in front of her, the man she knew nothing about other than the blind date disaster story. "Normal? You mean lots of people shake like this after finding their cars missing?"

"Sure, but I was referring to the aftereffects of the robbery." His rugged voice softened, and the unmistakable gentleness she heard made her heart suspend beating.

"You know about what happened?" She shook harder. There were the images again, piercing like sharpened blades into her thoughts, cutting through the present and making her remember. The ear-spitting thunder of gunfire, the rapid *pop-pop-pop* and the echoes resounding against the tile walls of the kitchen. The crash to the floor of a tub of dishes as Juanita dropped, falling like a rag doll.

Don't remember. She closed her eyes, drew in cold fresh air and thought of the passage from her morning's devotional. *Cast all your anxiety on Him because He cares for you.* The words calmed her. She let go of the images too painful to face.

"I'm a detective with the city police department," he explained, his hand gently settling on hers. His touch calmed her. "I was on the backdoor burglar case. I was assigned halfway through the investigation."

"You're a cop." When she opened her eyes, she saw understanding on his handsome, rugged face and more sympathy than she could accept. "I never would have guessed it."

"I'll take that as a compliment." Up close, his eyes were the truest blue she had ever seen. The tight grip in her stomach eased, the one that had been there since that fateful night when her world changed. For the first time in a long while she felt her muscles relax.

She looked at Max as if she'd never seen him before. In the shadowy light he looked surreal, more dream than flesh and blood. His essence shone through, with a noble heart and trustworthy goodness even she could believe in. "If you're a detective, then you must see a lot of the bad stuff. The dark side of humanity."

"I have." His hand on hers felt like a lifeline. "Sometimes, now and then, I see the bright side, too."

His smile made it seem as if he thought she was one of those bright sides. Warmth filled her until the cold, bad pieces lodged in her memories faded and she felt like the girl she used to be, full of wishes for the future without shadows. She breathed in the sweet evening air, made sweeter for the scent of his aftershave, and savored the sun on her face. It was good to be herself again before tragedy changed who she was.

She managed a carefree smile. "Mister, you are trying to charm the wrong woman."

"Hey, I'm not trying to charm you." He was pure innocence with a dash of trouble crooking his grin.

"You're just naturally charming?" she joked, but she was serious, too. "Thanks for coming to my rescue, but you should return to waiting for your date. I'm fine. I can take it from here."

"I'm sure you can, but the truth is my date isn't coming."

"She's not?"

"I've been officially stood up." He shrugged casually, as if it were no big deal. "She called my cell a few minutes ago. That's why I'm on my way home."

"I'm sorry."

"No biggie. I get rejected a lot." He winked.

"Me, too." It felt okay to confess it and even better that they had this in common. "Dating is hard. That's what no one tells you."

"And it doesn't seem to get easier. I try not to take it personally."

"How can you not?" That's exactly what she wanted to know. Her entire identity didn't revolve around getting married. No, that wasn't it at all. She had been evaluating her life lately, and she realized there was a lot that she wanted but didn't have. Closeness, connection, her own family, security. She had a heart full of love to give. Why not try to find love and change her life for the better?

She tugged his coat more closely around her, glad the shivering was easing. "When a date doesn't want to see you again, even if you don't like them, it feels personal."

"Tonight is the perfect example. Alice sounded nice enough, but she didn't want to know me. That would take more than a thirty-second conversation. She rejected me because of what she wanted. She has no idea who I really am."

No, but I have an idea. Bree looked down at his capable hand covering hers. Her heart gave a little flutter. He was a nice guy. Who wouldn't be looking for that? "Next you're going to say Billy ditched meeting me because of his own shortcomings."

"That's right. Everyone has them. It's part of being human. I say it's best to accept your own, that makes it a lot easier to accept other people's." His smile was part dream, part impossibility. "Now, tell me the truth. Are you feeling better?"

"Much." The quaking deep inside had calmed. The past was safely where it belonged and the memories buried. She withdrew her hand reluctantly from his and hopped to the ground. "I'm over the shock of seeing my car gone."

"What do you think you're doing?"

"I'm getting out of your truck so you can go on your way."

"If you think I'm going to leave you standing in the parking lot by yourself, you're wrong." He closed the door and leaned against it. "There's a cruiser on its way. They'll take your statement, you'll sign the report and that's it."

"Nothing scary about that. I'll be fine." She smiled shakily. "Great. Now you think I'm emotionally challenged."

"No, I don't like to leave a lady by herself when it's getting dark."

"My sister is five yards away. I'm not by myself." She set her chin. She was fragile, but strong.

At least that was his guess. She would have to be, to come back from the trauma she had. He had seen others who had gone through similar experiences and they had never found themselves again. He ached for them and likely for what lovely Brianna had gone through. The specifics were sketchy in his mind, since he'd gone on to other cases, but he remembered the string of burglaries that had grown more violent with each occurrence until three victims had been left dead and two others gravely injured. Violence happened, even in Montana.

"I'll stick around." He couldn't stop the pull of concern in his chest. "I want to make sure you have moral support if you need it."

"Thanks, but I don't want to be a burden. I've got my sister, if I need her."

He remembered. The waitress who had served his dessert had been a duplicate of Brianna. Twins. He studied the woman standing in front of him, framed by the rosy light of the setting sun. The cinch of emotion in his chest tugged harder. Odd, since she was all wrong for him. Way too wrong for a broken-down soul like him.

"Besides," she was saying in a gentle alto, "you don't want to hang around waiting for me to talk to the police. I'm sure a guy like you has a lot more exciting things to do."

"Sure. That's me. Excitement." Not. He got enough of that on the job. His pager buzzed, vibrating in his jeans pocket. He tugged it out not surprised to see that it was work calling. There was no rest for the weary and never for a detective. He would call in a little bit. He fastened his gaze on the woman with the wind scattering her long hair and with shadows on her face. First things first. He wasn't going to leave until—

A short burst of a siren shot out, and he looked up. It sure looked like trouble coming. Dobbs and Paulson, two buddies of his, pulled into the lot in an unmarked cruiser. He held up a hand, signaling them over.

"The cavalry has arrived." He wanted to stay, but she was no damsel in distress. She stood on her own feet, looking determined and only a little shaky.

The cruiser pulled to a stop and the window zipped down, revealing Dobbs and his know-it-all grin. Max shook his head. He knew what his good buddy was thinking, so he spoke first. "This is Brianna. Her car turned up missing."

The door swung open. "Is that so? Well, Brianna, let's take a report and see what we can do. We've had a lot of this kind of thing lately."

Max watched Brianna nod shyly at the officers. Her chin was set, but she was pale. She was struggling, but she didn't want it to show, that was his guess. She looked achingly vulnerable as she wrapped her arms around her middle and went to answer Dobbs's questions. He'd pulled his clipboard out of the car and was taking information. Max wasn't surprised to learn she worked at the bakery, since she was sugar and sweetness.

Remembering his page, he called in. Standing in the crisp March wind as the sun slid ever downward, he shivered. Maybe it was the damp air, or maybe it was something else. Something he didn't want to think about too hard. The call connected, the line rang and he waited, unable to rip his attention away from Brianna. The wind ruffled the rich light gold of her hair, gently tossing it against her silken face. With the light shimmering over her in the last long moments before the sun vanished, she looked like a fairy-tale princess, something too good to be real and impossible to believe in.

A voice came on the line—Fredericks. There was a shooting at the far end of town. Probably drug related. He pocketed the phone, conflicted. He had to leave. He didn't want to. Wasn't that always the way? The job came first. He liked what he did, and he had never found himself hesitating on answering a call. He had work, but what was he doing? Strolling toward the woman who took the pen Dobbs had offered her and signed her name with a flourish on the bottom of the clipboard.

He jammed his hands into his pockets and closed the short distance between them. "Do you need a ride, Brianna? I'd be happy to take you home."

Out of the corner of his eye he caught Dobbs's wide grin and a wink as he backed away to the cruiser. Apparently both uniforms were taking interest in the interaction. Great. Just what he needed, more ribbing from a bunch of married guys.

"I'll have my sister take me home. She gets off in a little while." She padded toward him, moving like poetry with the last of the day's light pearling her perfect face.

He didn't like that this was ending. He couldn't begin to explain why. He took a step toward her, just one step, that was all. Maybe it was best that he held his ground. "I guess this is goodbye."

"Yes." She shrugged out of his jacket with graceful movements and handed him the garment. "Here's hoping we both have better luck on our next blind dates."

"Sure." It was all he could think to say. Max Decker, the man who had a comeback for any occasion, stood speechless as she cast him one last look. Her gaze met his like a bolt of electricity and it jarred through his system, leaving him rooted to the spot.

Amazing. He watched as she glided away, unaware of what she'd done to him with one single glance. His heart had stopped beating. The blood stalled in his veins. He struggled for air as she walked away with her gentle, easy gait, her sleek straight hair brushing her shoulder blades with each step.

Why was he captivated? Was it sympathy for her or something more? She opened the door without looking back. He watched her sister look up and spot the patrol car, and dismay crossed her face. The sisters hugged, and from half a parking lot away, Max turned, tangled up with too many emotions to name.

"Was that your date?" Paulson had retreated to the driver's side of the car and was leaning on the edge of the roof, grinning knowingly. "She's real pretty. Too bad it had to end like that."

Max shook his head, but he didn't need to say a word. Dobbs was already answering.

"She *wasn't* Alice. It was my idea to set him up with Alice. So, what gives?"

"The same old thing. The lady wasn't looking to be a cop's wife." Who could blame her? He didn't. "I gotta go. Got a shooting across town. You jokers try not to get into trouble out there tonight."

"You know us. We're nothing but trouble." Dobbs winked, but there was no smile in his eyes. Their work was like that. They could kid around all they wanted, what they did was serious. "See ya, Decker."

Max nodded once, waiting until the cruiser had rolled before he took one last look at the bakery. Brianna was at a table toward the back, and all he could see of her was the cascading length of her blond hair and the curve of her back. Emotion tugged within him and he closed it down.

Time to go. He yanked open his truck door, realizing his coat was fisted in one hand. Brianna. He smelled her soft, sweet perfume on the garment, something gentle and innocent. Tenderness swept over him, tenderness he didn't want to feel.

Chapter Three

"Are you sure you're okay, Bree?"

"Fine." Sweat streaked down her spine, but other than that she was perfectly okay.

As she waited for her sister to take one look around the bakery's kitchen and make sure everything was in order and all appliances turned off, she reminded herself of how this night was different.

The moon was big and round, casting plenty of light to chase away the shadows around the back door. They weren't alone—all the other workers were waiting outside the door in the comforting glare of the security lights. It was March, not a hot summer night. Most of all, there was no gunman, no ricochet of bullets firing and no terror. She breathed in the fresh air, let the peace of the evening roll over her and faith reassure her.

"Then let's roll." Brandi gave the door a tug.

Glad to be leaving, Bree stepped into the back lot. There were goodbyes as the other two workers broke apart, heading off to their nearby cars. Everything was fine. There would be a day when she didn't worry so much, or feel as if the other shoe was about to drop.

"So that hunky guy is a detective, huh?" Brandi asked with just a tad too much of a smile.

Oh, she *so* knew what her twin was up to. She was trying to distract her from the memories. Really. "Don't start jumping to conclusions."

"Why not? He and that gorgeous woman he talked with never did wind up at the same table together. I happened to notice." Brandi grinned as she sorted through her keys to unlock the passenger door of her battered little pickup. The poor thing had seen much better days ten years ago. "He *could* like you."

"You are a meddler, sister dear."

"I know." Cheerfully, she opened the door and circled around to the driver's side. "He seemed awfully nice. Manly, you know, as in solid, strong, mature."

"Oh, I know." Did she! She could still feel the weight of his leather coat on her shoulders, warm from him and faintly pine scented. Nice. "He wasn't interested in me."

"How can you tell?"

"Uh, he didn't ask for my last name or my number." Not that she'd expected him to. She dropped onto the seat, slid her bag on the floor and banged the door shut. "This is the last time I'm going on a blind date."

"Be careful. You've said those words before." Brandi turned over the ignition and gave the truck gas, hoping the engine would catch. It rolled over and over. "Blind dates aren't so bad."

"How can you say that? They're terrible. Look at tonight. Disaster."

"Sure, but it *could* have been worse."

"How, exactly?"

"Uh, the building could have caught fire?" The engine finally caught and roughly idled. Brandi twisted in her seat to back out of the spot with a squeak of brakes and a whine from the transmission. "At least you met a nice guy. Okay, so he didn't want to date you, but at least you know nice guys are out there."

"As rare as hen's teeth, but they exist." Bree frowned, remembering how Max had made her feel. Small and dainty and utterly feminine, and incredibly, wonderfully safe. That was exactly how the right man ought to affect her.

Now, she simply had to find the right man for her. No easy task. "I mean it, I'm done with blind dates. Notice how you don't go on any?"

"Sure, because I'm not looking for Mr. Right. Believe me, I'm in no hurry to find out he doesn't exist."

Yikes, that was exactly what she was afraid of down deep. Beneath her optimistic thinking and her stubborn faith, that in the end, there would be no Mr. Right and no happiness. She sighed, pushing away the dark shadows from her childhood. "Although a girl has to have hope."

"Yes, and you keep holding on to it," her sister agreed. "And I will try to somehow. Despite my totally pessimistic attitude."

"Hey, careful. That's an attitude I'm trying not to catch."

"Which is why I'm keeping my opinions to myself."

Bree grinned. She could always count on her sister to be supportive, even if she didn't agree. Their family was broken and scattered, and she had half brothers and half sisters she hadn't seen in years. Mom had never been exactly what you could call reliable, and Dad, well, he'd been in and out of prison most of her life. Not exactly model parents or the kind a girl could ever depend on, which made her sister a double blessing.

The lights of Bozeman flashed by as they drove along in companionable silence. Despite the theft of her car and her no-show date, the evening didn't feel like a loss. She smiled, snuggled safely into the car's bucket seat, thinking about Max. Not that she would ever see him again—what were the chances?—but it didn't hurt to hold the memory of meeting him close, like her own little handful of a dream.

The headlights spotlighted their rented duplex, and the truck squeaked to a stop on the concrete driveway. As they pulled into the carport, reality set in. They were home. Tonight she had a lot to be thankful for—that the only thing taken from her was her car. Tomorrow there would be the insurance agent to call and transportation to figure out.

But as she opened the car door, she thought of Max and how he had offered her his coat. Memories of his kindness warmed her as she followed her sister inside, where the heater clicked on and she felt safe.

It was well past midnight, and he still couldn't get the young woman out of his mind. Max hit the garage door button, sorting through his keys while the door cranked shut. He unlocked his door, thinking of how she had looked standing alone in the light of sunset with his coat too big on her delicate frame.

Bree was an image of goodness and loveliness he wanted to believe in. But could he? He didn't like to admit it, but he'd lost his ability to believe in people. He was struggling to believe in a lot of things. The lock tumbled, he opened the door and stalked into his kitchen.

A single light over the sink shone, casting an amber glow across the marble countertops. Looked like his kid brother, whom he was raising, had done the dishes and cleaned up. Good kid. Marcus was in bed asleep, and the place felt empty.

The town house was something he'd picked up because it beat paying rent. He'd been here nine months and had yet to feel as if he'd come home. Maybe it was because he'd learned that nothing was permanent. He knew from on-the-job training that life could change in a blink; he didn't count on much lasting these days. He took one day at a time.

He pulled a can out of the refrigerator and popped the top. The lemony ice tea ran down his throat like comfort. He'd worked hard tonight. It felt good to mosey over into the living room, put his boots up on the coffee table and sit in the dark.

He was too wound up from his work to go up to bed; he wasn't in the mood for TV. He took another long swig of tea and tried to blot out the ugliness of the night. He couldn't forget the broken-down excuse for a house near the railroad tracks, children's chunky plastic toys scattered around the filthy floor where a gun had been discharged. He couldn't forget the father who was too high to realize where his toddler had wandered off to. They had found him playing on the tracks. It was a blessing no trains had ambled through. Social Services had been called, and now he would have another file of heartache on his desk.

The man who'd been arrested was the brother-in-law to the backdoor burglar, as fate would have it. Or, he believed more strongly, God.

Max set down his can with a clink in the stillness. It was the quietest time of night, when no traffic rolled by and it felt as if even the shadows slept. His feet hit the floor and he launched himself out of the chair, haunted by the image of Brianna when he'd first laid eyes on her. She had big violet eyes and the sweetest face. His chest tightened. He wanted to think it was only curiosity and nothing else that drove him upstairs past Marcus's room, where he opened the door a crack—yep, the kid was asleep. He wandered into the second bedroom and saw his computer glowing in the corner.

Sure, maybe it was more than a little curiosity, he conceded as he logged in and found the local newspaper's Web site. He typed in his password, remembering when he'd first approached Brianna's table and how she'd smiled up at him. He punched a few keys and hit Search, waiting, recalling how hard he'd been hoping that the nice-looking blonde could possibly be his blind date. And praying equally as hard she wasn't.

And why? Going out to meet Alice hadn't been his idea. After six months of pressure, he'd finally caved. That was all there was to it. He wasn't a blind-date kind of guy. He'd gone to shut his buddies up, that was it.

Okay, maybe there was still a little bit of hope alive in him somewhere that he would find the right woman. That there would be that click, and life could turn for the better.

The screen changed, offering him several links to articles. He hit the last headline and waited. Several grainy black-and-white images crowded the screen with a long front-page article on the holdup. Two kitchen workers and a cook dead, and a waitress taken by medevac to Seattle's Harborview Hospital. Brianna.

With his heart thundering, he scrolled down the screen and skimmed the article. He wanted to see the specifics of the case again in black-and-white. His eyes caught the phrase "…waitress in critical condition. Charles Lintle, the restaurant's dishwasher, said Miss McKaslin ran to the aid of her fallen coworker without regard for her own safety. That she was injured while trying to save a life seems doubly cruel…."

Max squeezed his eyes shut, unable to read more. A sick feeling filled his gut. Sympathy left him trembling. This was why he believed in his work, and why he gave his job all he had. He did his best to catch the bad guys before they could hurt more innocent people. But it was never enough, never fast enough.

He breathed air into his strangling lungs and bowed his head for a quick prayer of gratitude. However badly she was hurt, Brianna had recovered. At least physically. He thanked the Lord for that. The image of her shivering in the parking lot looking alone and vulnerable lingered, getting him right in the soul.

When he opened his eyes, he read no more. He got off-line, shut off the monitor and wandered through the darkness down the hall. His room was dark, too. Cold inside, he flipped on the lamp and reached for the top book on a big stack on the nightstand. The comforting feel of his Bible felt good in his hands. It had been a long day.

The mattress faintly squeaked as he sat on the

edge and opened the guide to the marked page. *If I take the wings of the dawn, if I dwell in the remotest part of the sea, even there Thy hand will lead me, and Thy right hand will lay hold of me.*

He took comfort in the truth that God was watching over them all, that no sorrow went un-noticed, and no valor.

Brianna stayed on his mind as he sat in the dark, listening to the hours pass.

She woke from the nightmare right before she screamed Juanita's name. Bathed in sweat, her stomach knotted up with horror and hopeless failure. With her blood thick in her veins, she sat up in bed, blinking, fighting to reorient herself. Gradually the echoing explo-sions of gunfire faded, the scent of bleach and cooked food evaporated and the vision of injury and death lessened. She groped for the bedside lamp, knocking over knickknacks on the night-stand, and finally found the switch. A small pool of light flashed on, chasing away some of the darkness. A lot of shadows remained.

The shadows were huge tonight, like living monsters ready to hurl her back into the past. A place she never wanted to revisit. She swal-lowed against the metallic taste of fear on her tongue and pulled her Bible into her arms. She closed her eyes and recited the Lord's Prayer until her pulse returned to normal and the memories no longer threatened.

But would they ever go away entirely? She prayed they would, but tonight they clung stubbornly to her soul. Maybe having her car stolen had shaken her more than she'd thought. It had been just a car, a possession, a thing that could not be injured or die, nothing that her insurance couldn't replace, but the crime had shaken her all over again. A reminder that in an instant, life could change.

Just breathe, she ordered. She closed her eyes and drew in a slow, deep breath, trying to feel it all the way to her toes, and then slowly released it. In came the good air, out went the bad feelings. Her counselor insisted it helped, but when she stopped, twenty breaths later, she was mostly light-headed. The fears lurked like danger in the dark.

She was perfectly safe. Her second-story bedroom window was hard to climb into, and the locks on the doors were good ones. She was stronger than the fear, stronger than the men who had broken into the restaurant and who haunted her still.

Okay, she was still trembling. That was not good. No way was she going to be able to go back to sleep like this. She didn't dare look at the clock, in case her mind would start zeroing in on the time. Another thing to make it harder to relax, let go and fall into vulnerable sleep.

Reading often helped, but she wasn't going to pick up her inspirational romance book. No, because she would start reading about the hero in the book and that would remind her of Max. Remembering how kind he had been, giving her his coat and sitting her in his truck made the emptiness in her room expand.

No, she would turn to a love she did have. She flipped open her Bible to the bookmark and found her place on the page. *The thief does not come except to steal, and to kill, and to destroy. I have come that they may have life, and that they may have it more abundantly.*

It was a great comfort to know that God never intended for that robbery to happen. But that His good would triumph, and she had to hold on. The nightmares would fade in time and so would the pain. God's gift of life and love were ahead of her. She had faith.

Thank goodness, her pulse had returned to normal, although now she was wide awake. The shadows remained, so she slipped out of bed, careful not to squeak the floorboards and wake up Brandi in the next room. She woke up her laptop and logged on. She could do a little library research. That was dry enough to definitely put her in a sleepy mood.

But did she go directly to the university's library site like she was supposed to? No. She noticed a new e-mail in her Inbox. Reading mail was always much better than finding reference books on phonics versus word recognition teaching methods.

The e-mail was from her half brother Luke. She clicked on it, eager to read the letter entitled "Howdy!"

Hey, Bree,

I was in town today picking up feed and supplies for the farm. Hoped to get a chance to call you and Brandi, but not hardly. Too much to do, too little time, a temperamental pickup. You know how it is. Hunter came with me, and he's my brother and all, but he was in an especially sour mood. No news there, right?

A smile warmed her. She could hear Luke's easy country cadence gently ribbing their older brother. They farmed land from their mother's side of the family an hour's drive from the city. She hadn't grown up knowing her brothers, but after her hospital stay, they had kept in touch. Luke especially, who spent a lot of evenings on his computer.

I've got two things on my mind. One—I know your trial is coming up in seven, or is it eight weeks? I'm not near a calendar. Anyway, we're planning on coming down to be with you. Let us know the schedule in advance, if you can. I don't know how the courts and lawyers do it, but any warning would make it easier on us here. We've got livestock and crops to consider, and we want to be there for you, kiddo.

The trial. Bree took a deep breath. In with the good, out with the bad. But the shadows remained. She dreaded having to relive it all over again. She hated that she was going to have to testify and look at the surviving gunman, who would be sitting beside his lawyers looking innocent and misunderstood. When she knew the truth—the weight of Juanita's limp body as she fought to clear an air passage, his violent shouting about wanting all of the money.

Take another deep breath, Bree. She closed her eyes until the memories silenced. One day all of this would be in the past. One day she would say this experience, as bad as it was, strengthened her in spirit and in faith. It taught her how much she had wanted to survive her injuries, how much she loved her life.

I've been e-mailing with Brooke, and I've got her halfway talked into coming back home 'round that time for a visit. That sister of ours is having a hard time, but won't admit it. How did the blind date turn out? If you're interested, I know someone I could set you up with.

Great. Double great. Another blind date. Why, when what were the chances she'd meet someone as perfect as Max? Although she had tried to stop thinking about him, he rushed into her thoughts. If only she could forget his stunning blue eyes, unassuming humor and manly tenderness. Or how he'd draped his coat around her shoulders like any romantic hero would, or that a girl could get lost in the deep comforting rumble of his voice.

You weren't going to go there, right? She turned her attention back to the computer screen.

The other thing I've got to mention to you. I got a letter from Dad. Yes, he's still in prison, but he's coming up for parole. He wanted to borrow money. No surprise there, but heads up. He might be contacting you or Brandi next. Take care, little sister. Write when you can.

Luke

Dad. Up for parole. That was nothing but trouble. Brianna's stomach cinched up into an impossibly tight knot. How old did you have to be until your past stopped mattering? Until the wounds of your childhood stopping hurting?

She didn't have any answers to that. She had stopped counting on her dad a long time ago, but his sins seemed to cling to her, part of the shadows, too. Those shadows dimmed the brightness, every last thought of Max and the hopes she had for her life.

It was a long time until the darkness thinned and the shadows eased. Only then could she sleep.

Chapter Four

"Heard you bombed out big-time with that classy woman Dobbs set you up with." His little brother took a shot and the basketball swooshed through the net—a perfect two points. Marcus pumped his fist in the air. "All right! I'm up four points on you now, old man."

"Watch who you're calling old." His growl was more bark than bite, but it was tradition between the two of them. "You got in a few lucky shots is all."

"It's not luck. It's called *skill*." Marcus hopped after the ball and tossed it into the court. The echoing ruckus from the other one-on-one games bounced around the cavernous downtown gym.

Max caught the ball, enjoying their good-natured banter. Hanging out with his bro was number one on his list of favorite activities.

"It's called *false hope,* because I'm going to make the next three baskets. Watch and learn."

"Pathetic." Marcus's basketball shoes squeaked on the varnished floor as he tried blocking.

The kid was good, which was one reason why Max had given notice, packed his possessions and moved him from California to Montana. Not an easy transition for a man born and bred in the heart of the city, but worth it. He shot, he scored, and it was his turn to pump his fist. "You're only ahead by one basket, hot shot."

"I'm not worried." He dribbled the ball like a pro, loping with his long stride toward the basket.

"You'd better be worried." Max blocked, stealing the ball and dropping it through the net. "Who's the king now?"

"The game's not over, bro." The kid grabbed the ball, dribbling, setting up a nice layup and the shrill note of a whistle cut through the boy's concentration.

"Time to pack it up for the night," the pastor, who oversaw the youth program, called above the noise. While groans and protests rang out, the gym full of teens stopped their games and began tossing their basketballs into the cans near the back door.

"Saved by the whistle." Max tapped the ball,

knocked it out of the kid's grip and gave it a toss. It sailed into the end basket, neatly missing everyone, and into the bin. "Another two points for me."

"Sad. I feel sorry for you. The only way you can beat me is to cheat." Marcus winked, although he shook his head, feigning sympathy. "It only proves it. You're washed up. Obsolete. It's a wonder the police department doesn't retire you. Can't even beat a kid at basketball."

"I'm pathetic, I know, but next week, watch out." The kid was good. And if things kept going as they were, he would graduate high school at the top of his class with a college scholarship in hand. They walked to the bleachers, keeping the conversation up as they pulled sweatpants over their workout clothes. Zipping up jackets, they headed out the door into the surprisingly cold evening.

"Loser buys the pizza, so it'll be your turn to treat. Again." Marcus held out his hand to check the falling chunks of precipitation, for it was amazingly white. "Is that snow? Man, I can't believe this place. I miss L.A."

"Tell it to the weatherman." Personally, he didn't care if it snowed all year long. All that mattered was that Marcus was in a good environment, doing well in school and keeping his nose clean. He beeped the remote and his truck's door locks snapped open.

"Hand over the keys, bro." The kid's palm shot out. "I won. I get to drive."

"You played a good game, Marcus." Max hadn't grown up in a touchy-feely home but he handed over the keys, sure the boy would understand that the gesture was meant to be affectionate. "Don't you chip my paint job, you hear?"

"Sweet." Ignoring the warning, the kid loped toward the driver's side. "I wish I had a rig."

"That money in your account at the bank is for college. Not a truck. End of story."

"Yeah, I know. I get it."

Hiding a grin, Max hopped into the passenger seat and buckled in. He was glad he'd come with his brother tonight. Being busy kept his mind off of certain subjects—work and, more troubling, Brianna McKaslin. Ever since he'd stayed up most of the night after reading that newspaper article, she'd taken up residence in his head. Days had passed, and he couldn't explain why. She didn't belong there.

That didn't stop him from remembering how she'd looked in the bakery. His first sight of her had been a mix of "wow" and "oh no." She was too naive, too young, too perfect, too sweet for him. Her voice had been low and musical, a quiet melody that he wanted to hear again. He wasn't a complicated man, and he knew what he felt was interest. She had the prettiest eyes he had ever seen.

"Hey, bro. Are you paying attention?" Marcus called out, sounding amused.

Max shook his head. "Sorry, I was off thinking."

"For about four whole minutes."

That was the truth. He glanced around, realizing they were already out of the snowy parking lot and on one of the main roads, where the traffic kept the streets wet, with only a slight layer of white up the center of the lanes.

"Look at that poor person." Marcus nodded once, gesturing toward the upcoming block where a bike's reflective taillight flashed amid the stubbornly falling snow. "Someone really needs a car. That can't be pleasant. It's freezing out there."

"Freezing," Max agreed, staring at the biker.

It was too dark to recognize anyone, much less from behind. The rider was diminutive, slender of shoulders and of frame, but it was hard to see much more than that. He spotted light reflected off the helmet, but that's all the information he could gather. He moved in his seat and gave the shoulder harness a tug. It felt suddenly tight against his chest. Why did his heart stop beating? Why was he struggling for air? The last time he'd gotten the identical feeling, it had been watching Brianna Mc-Kaslin walk away from him.

Better planning, Bree told herself as she stopped for the red light. That's all it would have taken, but oh no, she had been sure she could make the twenty-minute bike ride from the library on campus to the bookstore. She should have foreseen disaster. Planned for delays. For getting caught behind the bus. And snow, she added when a white flake caught on her eyelash.

Only six more blocks. She hated the shadows that seemed to hide all kinds of danger. She wished her nerve endings would stop popping and her pulse would stop thudding in her ears with the decibel level of a marching band. Cars swished by in the opposing lanes, headlights glaring as they swung to make left-hand turns. She shivered, vulnerable on her bike.

You're fine, Bree. Everything's fine. The road is well lit. You're going to be okay. Doom is not right around the corner. She glanced to her left and right, wanting to be aware of her environment. A pair of students, with backpacks slung over their shoulders, walked along the sidewalk on the other side of the street. Light spilled from the streetlight above, and the parking lot paralleling the road was busy with people. Students piled out of cars or carried pizza in boxes back to their vehicles, and shoppers walked along the specialty shops browsing.

No reason to panic. She shook snow off her bike helmet, wiped her eyes with her sleeve and focused on the light overhead. Okay, it could turn any time now. Once she was moving, she would feel less vulnerable.

A big white truck pulled up in the lane beside her. No big deal. Except for the fact that the passenger window began to roll down. Great. It was going to be all right, even if she didn't recognize the truck.

Wait. Or did she? There was something at the back of her mind, a memory just out of reach. Recognition bolted through her like lightning. Max. It looked like his truck. And, the man shadowed in the interior of the truck looked remarkably like him, too.

"What are you doing out here in this?" Max Decker hung out the window, clearly undaunted by the cold and the pummeling snow.

It wasn't relief that zipped through her like a funnel cloud. No, it was something much more troubling. "Hey, detective. I didn't think I would ever see you again."

"Haven't been on a blind date lately." His lopsided grin could have been a movie star's. "What are you doing out in this weather?" he repeated.

"My stolen car hasn't turned up yet." She couldn't help feeling like a doofus. *Hel-lo?* Max had a lot going for him—and she so didn't, the proof being she was on her old ten-speed. "I didn't go for the rental-car part of the policy, so here I am, biking it."

"Can we give you a lift? This is Marcus, my little brother. Half brother, really, but I'm stuck with him the same as if he was the real thing." He winked, obviously joking. The teenager behind the wheel gave a "Hey!" in good-natured protest.

So, a new piece of the puzzle that was Max Decker. Interesting. Brianna swiped another snowflake from her eye and noticed the light had changed. Green glowed in the falling snow as she waved off his offer. No cars had pulled in behind them so she had time to answer. "Thanks, but I only have six blocks to go."

"Six blocks, huh?" He glanced down the street, thoughtful and unruffled. "Six block up, there's another shopping mall. You can't live there."

"No, but my sister works there. My half sister, since we're being specific." She couldn't help the smile tugging at the corners of her mouth. Was she flirting with him?

Most of all, was he flirting with her?

No, he couldn't be. No way. She gripped both handlebars securely, both ready to kick off and unable to move.

"It's snowing harder." His tranquil observation forced her to notice the pummeling flakes now falling as if they were hail. *Tap, tap, tap* on the street, obscuring the road ahead. *Thump, thump, thump* on her helmet. His door swung open and he hopped to the ground. "Looks like the weather's getting serious. Stow your bike in the back. Go on, get up in there."

"But, it's only six blocks."

"Just do it." His order was softened by something in his voice. Concern. Caring. Interest?

No, that was just her hopes talking. "It's my policy not to take orders from domineering men."

"Every policy has got to be broken some time." He planted one capable hand in the middle of the handlebars, holding the contraption steady. "Go on, climb in. It's warm in the truck. Shelter from the storm."

Yeah, she knew all about that. The intense blue glint in his eyes and the tug of amusement at the corner of his mouth and his commanding presence made her weak. Too weak. She had an independent streak a mile wide, but it shrank to nothing as she swung off the bike.

"Marcus, turn on the hazards, would ya?" He lifted it easily, hauled it after them and opened the door for her. "And amp up the defroster."

"Aye, aye, captain."

Bree caught an impression of a strong-featured teenager—a shock of dark hair and mocking deep blue eyes—before she plopped onto the seat. Max remained at her side, riveting her attention, filling her senses: the crisp scent of the snowy night, the dark hint of a five-o'clock shadow on his strong jaw, the vibration of his voice and the heat radiating off him as he leaned close.

Stop noticing, Bree, she instructed, but did she comply? Impossible.

"Brianna, meet Marcus. Kid, you be nice to the lady until I get back."

"We're still going for pizza, aren't we?" The teenager looked alarmed.

"Food. It's all he thinks about." Max shook his head, winked at her and closed the door.

Warmth cradled her as the heater blasted over her face. As she struggled with her helmet straps and snow tumbled onto her lap, onto the seat, onto the floor. She shivered. Apparently she hadn't realized she was a walking, talking, biking human icicle until Max had stepped away from her. Proof that she was way too hung up on the man.

Try a little dignity, huh? She blushed, realizing the brother was watching her. He was a big kid, wide-set the way Max was, and sharp-eyed. He hadn't missed a thing.

"He's not bad. Wanna go to eat with us? We're gettin' pizza."

The back door of the crew cab swung open. "No, kid, she probably doesn't want to get pizza with us. You don't have to feel obligated, Bree."

"Oh, I don't—"

Marcus piped in. "Did you eat yet?"

"Well, no I—"

"Then you should come with us." The kid grinned into the rearview mirror, as if he thought himself pretty smart. "The lady gets to pick the pizza toppings."

"You don't have to say yes, Brianna." Max snapped his seat belt into place. "You might have something better to do with your sister."

"Actually, I'm hanging out until she's done working to get a ride home." She twisted in the seat, peering over the headrest at him.

"You aren't saying no?" He wanted to be sure he got that right.

"I'm not saying no. It's tempting." She settled back against the seat as the truck ambled through the intersection. "But I have a fondness for pepperoni."

Now he had to like her. He had a weakness for pepperoni—and nothing else. "How much longer do you have to go car-less?"

"The insurance company says they will issue a check next week, but you know how that goes."

"Do I." He buckled in but couldn't relax. He felt on edge, but not in a bad way. Brianna was the reason. Everything about her drew him in, from the melting snow glistening like diamonds in her golden hair, to her sweet lilac scent, to the sound of her whispering sigh as she held her hands up to the heater vent, as if grateful.

Still that innocent storybook princess.

Anything that appeared too good to be true, had to be. That was his experience. That was the way the world worked. But so help him, when he looked at her he never wanted anything to be truer. He wanted Brianna to be everything she seemed to be and more.

Sad, but there it was. He didn't like that she had been out biking in the snow. "It isn't as if you are the only biker out there tonight." He tapped on the window for emphasis when they came across another one, although this biker was a man who looked hard core, as if he biked year-round regardless of the weather. "It's the best you could do for transportation?"

"Yes, for tonight, at least. My sisters are working, my friends are all occupied elsewhere for one reason or another, so the bike was the last resort." She ran her fingers through her hair, combing out the melting diamonds. "I was supposed to be at the bookstore an hour ago, that's where Colbie works—"

"Colbie is the one who set you up with the nose-ring guy."

"Right. Anyway, I got stuck talking to a professor after class, there was a line ahead of me and I thought, this won't take that long. I'll be fine. Wrong. Then I saw someone I knew on campus. I figured it wouldn't take long to stop and say hi. Wrong. When I finally got on my way, I got caught behind the bus. Five red lights and four bus stops. It all adds up to me riding home in the dark in the snow."

"Perfect timing for us, though." Max rapped his knuckles against his brother's shoulder and pointed left. "Use the turn signal."

"Yeah, yeah." Marcus rolled his eyes, but the kid was grinning. He obviously enjoyed giving his older brother guff.

"Here we are." Max seemed relieved his brother had delivered them all safely. "You need to call that sister of yours?"

"No, I texted her to say I was running late when I was stuck behind the bus for two of the five red lights."

"So, you've got two sisters?"

"No. Besides, Brandi and Colbie, I also have a sister and two brothers from my dad's first marriage."

"I have a family like that. Halves and wholes, scattered all over the place. My dad was a cop. Being a cop is tough on a marriage. Very tough." That hurt, but it was only the truth. It wasn't as if he had a chance with her. It wasn't as if he wanted to, right? At least, that's the way it had to be. "It's why I haven't shackled myself in holy bonds."

"Then why were you on a blind date?"

"I guess some hopes spring eternal, however small." That was only the truth. Good thing the truck rolled to a stop in a prime spot next to the curb, and Marcus killed the engine. Max didn't want to think too hard on the coincidence of running into her again. He couldn't say he hadn't been tempted to drop by the bakery on the chance that she would be working there. Just like he couldn't deny he hadn't been thinking about the backdoor burglar case and what she'd been through, the valor she had shown under fire.

He hopped out, got her door and took her

gloved hand to help her down. Nice, being near her. Cozy. He couldn't say he didn't notice when she smiled at him, her big violet-blue eyes captivating.

Good thing he was immune to captivating. Or a tough guy like him was supposed to be. He stayed at her side, protecting her from the wind and snow the best he could. He began to think stopping to pick her up had been a bad idea. Especially when she slipped through the door ahead of him, as dainty as royalty, yet as down to earth as could be in her winter jacket and worn jeans. Her suede boots padded on the tile floor ahead of him. Snow had caught in her hair again, dappling her as if with precious gems.

"Look. It's buffet night. My favorite." She tossed a smile over her shoulder, a simple gesture, innocent, as if wholly unaware of her power at that moment.

One glance, one smile, one word from her, his chest tightened and it was as if she'd looped a noose around his heart and had pulled it tight. How it happened, Max didn't know. The bright lights of the pizza parlor seemed tacky compared to her gentle grace as she stepped into line at the counter, drawing him along by the strings of his heart.

Boy, he was in trouble. Big-time.

Chapter Five

She was in trouble. Big-time. Bree knew it the moment she felt her phone vibrate in her coat pocket and chose to ignore it. She had sent Colbie a text message when she'd been standing in the long line at the counter, so it wasn't her big sister worrying over her. Whoever was calling her would have to wait— a first for her. But then, she had never been out with Max before. Not that you could call loading up on pizza, salad and cheese sticks an official date or anything.

You wish, Bree. She mentally rolled her eyes, because it was the truth. She wished this *was* a date. She wished Max would like her that way. But did she have a chance of that? Hardly. It wasn't as if he spent most of the time gazing into her eyes, making her feel as if she were the only person in the restaurant. It wasn't as if their talk had turned personal, like the way dates usually went.

He's years older than you, for one. She took a bite of pizza and savored the greasy-cheesy-pepperoni taste. He's really different from you, for another. She glanced through her lashes at Max, seated across the table, as he dug through his pockets for change.

"I'll take the nickels and dimes, too." Marcus cupped his hands. "How many dollar bills have ya got?"

"You're not getting my ones." Max shook his head, acting gruff but his eyes said otherwise. He had amazing eyes. Dark and deep and warm. Caring. "That's all I got. Now go play. Get out of my hair."

"Yeah, yeah." Marcus grinned, pocketed his change and grabbed his plastic soda cup. "A guy gets thirsty playing video games. See you two later."

The teenager loped away, his pockets rattling with money.

"That kid. Nothing but trouble." Max appeared disgruntled, but she knew better. It wasn't hard to see how deeply he cared.

She liked that about him. "You spend a lot of time with your little brother."

"Some." He gathered up a slice of pizza from his plate. "Family. What else are you going to do with them? You can give in and spend time with them or take your phone off the hook. Keep your doors locked. Never answer your e-mail."

Only the wry grin at the corners of his mouth gave him away. She liked that he was tough on the outside and a good-hearted man inside. She sipped her soda thoughtfully. "I know what you mean. There goes my phone, ringing again. Family."

"Are they mostly here in Bozeman?"

"Or nearby." She thought of the small town to the east where she and Brandi had grown up. Her mother had moved many times since and now lived only thirty minutes away, but it might as well have been a light-year.

"Must be nice having everyone close." He glanced past her, just like he had been doing through the entire meal, and stared at something beyond her shoulder. Probably his brother in the games corner. "I've got a sister in Fresno, a half sister in Florida, a sister by marriage in Anchorage and another half brother in Boston."

"My family may be here in Montana, but we're not as close as you might think."

"They live all over the state, huh?"

"No, that's not the close I meant." She thought of the yawning gulf that divided her family, the years and hardships. It was complicated. "When

Brandi and I moved to Bozeman to go to school, Lil heard about it and invited us to Sunday dinner. That's when we got to know Colbie and Lil better. But my brothers and Brooke, we're trying. We didn't grow up together."

There was so much a guy as solid as Max might not want to hear. Things that reminded her of the disadvantaged girl she'd been. She could still hear the neighbors talking at church, not realizing she'd been nearby. *What chance do those girls have, with parents like that? They'll be alcoholics before their tenth birthday.*

Ashamed, she pushed those memories away. "When I woke up in I.C.U., the nurses told me that all my sisters and brothers had spent the night in the waiting room praying for me. It was the first time we were all together in the same place. We're not exactly the perfect family."

"Don't worry. Neither was mine. My dad was always working. He was a detective with the L.A.P.D." His voice grew rougher with emotion and sorrow he did not explain. "It was a tough job. It changed him. Made him rough and bitter. I can't say the same thing hasn't happened to me, but I'm trying not to make his mistakes."

"I know how hard fighting bitterness can be. What were his mistakes?"

"Depression, post-traumatic stress. His marriage failed, so he got married again and that failed."

"Failed marriages are a tradition in my family, too." She could have said more, she wanted to say more, but she didn't. Max's integrity and strength made her hold back. She didn't know how he would react if she told him about her father. The truth was, she didn't want Max to know that about her dad. She did not come from a line of policemen. Her dad was a felon. Her mom drank too much and liked men who did the same. That was her legacy. "How old were you when your parents divorced?"

"Ten. It was tough." He stared down at his soda, seizing the cup with both hands. "He died in the line of duty when I was in the academy. Complications from a gunshot wound. A blood clot took him, when some of the toughest criminals in L.A. couldn't."

"I'm sorry. That had to be very hard for you."

"For Marcus more than me. He was a little kid. That was a long time ago." He swiped his face, obviously fighting emotion. "To answer your first question, yes, I spend a lot of time with him. He lives with me."

"You're raising him?"

"Shocking, I know. What do I know about a kid?" He shook his head, a smile hooking the left corner of his mouth and sadness making his eyes fathomless. "He got to be a handful for his mom. She had enough problems of her own, so I took him. The problems continued, so I scouted around for jobs outside of L.A. Got lucky when there was an opening here."

"Let me guess. You moved here last summer?"

"That would be an affirmative."

"That was why you came in on the tail end of my case." She understood now. He'd been new to the area. She considered him, this man who raised his younger half brother, who had moved away from everything he'd known for the boy's sake. Hard to disguise the sigh of respect rising through her. "Do you like Montana?"

"It has its high points." He polished off his soda. "What about you?"

"Me? I've never been out of the state. Maybe one day, but when I finish my degree, I want to teach in the area."

"Oh, so that's what you want to be." He took another bite of pizza. "A teacher?"

"One more semester and then it's student teaching. I'm nervous about that."

"You'll be fine." He was sure. He could see her in a classroom. "Are you talking high school, or do you want to teach the little tykes?"

"The little guys. I'm getting my degree in

elementary education." She took a dainty sip of soda. "I'm not sure about a job, though. Openings aren't that easy to find these days."

"Tell me about it. I looked for over a year until this one popped up. Even then, there were a lot of other guys applying." He took his cup and stood. "I have a good feeling about you, and I'm always right. You aren't going to have any trouble finding the right job."

"Your words to God's ears."

He had to believe that God was keeping special watch over her. The images of the crime scene flashed across his vision, the carnage and destruction. The lives forever lost. She had survived that and she sat before him looking untouched by it.

There had to be more to her story. She wasn't what she seemed. She *couldn't* be. He held out his hand for her cup. "Want another root beer?"

"Please."

"Thought I would snag a few slices of dessert pizza, too. Interested?"

"Always. I have a fondness for the cherry kind."

"Roger that." He took her cup, and his fingers bumped against hers. A shock jittered through his system with enough force to knock out his knees. No emotion had ever hit him like that before. He walked away on unsteady legs.

He wasn't going to let himself feel the tenderness gathering within him. He wasn't going to believe in what might never be.

At the soda dispenser, he glanced over his shoulder at the woman. She bent over her phone, thumbs flying as she texted, looking like his most secret, deepest dream. God sure had a sense of humor bringing her into his path. A fresh-faced, golden girl-next-door type.

She wasn't right for him, either. He thought of his dad and his unhappy marriages. He thought of all the ways his long hours and tougher personality would disappoint a woman like her. Every day he felt tainted by his job, saw more despair, touched evil. It was bound to rub off. To change a man.

This wasn't a date. He shouldn't forget that. He could make a list a mile long with all the reasons why he'd be better off not seeing her again. The kid had invited her. She was simply tagging along. That's how he had to think of this. He wanted to make sure she had a warm ride to her sister, that was all. That's as far as he could afford to let himself care.

But the lasso around his heart tugged a notch tighter.

He's looking for someone much different from me. Brianna continued her list as the truck rolled through the snowy streets with Max behind the wheel. He might not have said it, but he didn't have to. An image of the woman in the bakery that night came to her—polished, put together.

That's definitely the last thing I am. Sitting in the passenger seat with snowflakes batting at the windshield, she felt every flaw sharply, as if a spotlight were shining down on each one. It was simple reality. She was too short, too clueless, too burdened and with too many problems—the post-traumatic stress was a biggie. No wonder she was still single. She wouldn't date herself, either, if she was a guy.

But did that mean love only happened when you were tall enough, had enough sophistication and savvy or had worked out every problem with years of psychotherapy? That didn't make any sense, either.

"Is this the place?" Max bit out into the silence.

Bree took a look around, realizing they were in the parking lot where Colbie worked. "Yes. Thanks. You can just let me off at the front door."

"Just let you off, huh? As in dump you out?" Trouble, that's what it was, twinkling in his dark blue eyes. "Sorry. I'm not that kind of guy."

"Sweet," came Marcus's voice from the

backseat. "A bookstore. There's this book I want to get...."

"No one is talking to you right now." Max glanced into the rearview, but his smile hooked his dimples, and the teenager laughed. "You keep quiet, kid."

"Sure. I get it. I didn't know, bro." Marcus sounded amused.

Must be an inside joke. Whatever the two brothers were talking about, she hoped her own little secret wasn't about to be exposed. She unhooked her seat belt, hoping she wasn't blushing again. So, she liked Max. Really liked him. What girl wouldn't? It wasn't as if this was a date or anything. Her being with him was simply happenstance. Just one of those coincidences in life.

Her passenger door swung open. Max stood in the storm, hand out, to help her down. Could she help it if those tiny wishes glimmered to life when her hand met his? It was as if her heart whispered, this is The One.

Time stilled, and she felt weightless as she slipped off the seat. Snow tumbled from the heavens, sifting through the fall of light from the storefront and each flake shimmered. It fell over them both like grace, like a moment of pure blessing. Her doubts vanished, her worries fell away. There was only Max's riveting gaze and his strength radiating through her hand. Her feet hit the ground and although he moved away, the connection remained.

"Where do you want your bike?" Max asked as he shut the truck door.

"Oh, I'll go ahead and take it around back. I—"

"That wasn't what I asked." Firmly spoken, but his words resonated with kindness. "Go in where it's warm. I'll take the bike around back. Is there a rack there? Do you want it locked?"

"No, you can just lean it up against the side of the building. I'll load it later."

"Load it where?"

"On my sister's car. Do you have to know everything, Mr. Detective?"

"Yes. Yes I do." His dimples dug deep as he swung open the front door and held it for her.

Triple wow. He had that charisma thing going for him, and combined with the world-weary-hero thing, she felt completely overwhelmed. She slipped past him, aware of his height and his character. He was a total twenty on a scale of ten. A complete Mr. Dreamy. More so now that she'd gotten to know him better, the devoted cop, the loyal brother, one of the good guys.

Why couldn't she have met him before the robbery? As she retreated into the store's cozy warmth, her every flaw felt enormous. No matter how she fought it, her nose was too big, her legs were too short, she wasn't pretty enough, she was dealing with problems. Her hair was a mess, tangled from the driving wind and blotchy with melting snow.

Standing alone in the store's foyer with displays on either side of her, she was acutely aware of her consignment-store jeans and coat and outlet-store boots. Aware of the fears she hadn't been able to defeat since the night she'd been shot by a man on meth.

Her heart might be whispering, "He's The One," but her brain was definitely shouting, "Be realistic." For the second time, she would be saying goodbye to him, just like after the blind-date fiasco, and he would walk away for good. There would be no more chance encounters to bring them together, especially since she should be getting her insurance check soon. Which meant she would be a car owner again. If they did happen to meet on the road, they would both just keep driving, right?

When Max retreated into the storm, the shroud of snow stole him from her sight, and it was as if he had taken something from her. Something she couldn't name. She had never felt like this before with any guy.

Then again, she had never spent much time with a man like Max.

"Who is Mr. Handsome?" Colbie appeared between the rows of polished wood bookshelves. Curiosity animated her dear features— a heart-shaped face, to-die-for cheekbones, a perfect slope of a nose and big navy-blue eyes. She tucked a lock of light brown hair behind her ear. "Now I get why you suddenly decided to stop for dinner. Are you dating him?"

Bree held up one finger to her lips, wincing. The store was quiet, and there was no way Marcus could miss hearing everything, wherever he was in the store. "Max just gave me a ride. I met him when my car was stolen."

"Still, he's promising. I'm going to put him on my prayer list."

"Don't torture me like that." She gave her sister a quick hug, careful not to get her all snowy.

"Look at you. You're a mess!" No truer words had been spoken. "Now come here. Sit down where it's warm. This chair gets the breeze from the heater vent. I'll pour you some tea."

"You're not waiting on me." She dropped her backpack on the floor by one of the chairs and followed her sister to the beverage cart. Canisters towered neatly above a colorful arrangement of decorated cookies from the bakery. She grabbed two paper cups before Colbie could and filled both with steamy water.

"Did you get an e-mail from Luke about Dad?" Colbie's voice dropped low. Unhappiness pinched her pretty face. She busily chose two tea bags and dropped them in the cups of water.

"Yes. I thought we were through with all that." Bree's stomach bunched up. See? This was probably a sign from above. As much as she didn't want to look back and let her past dictate her future, she was forced to. After years of silence, the letters and phone calls were starting again. "He probably just wants money."

"Like we're all so flush." Colbie rolled her eyes, as if trying to make light of something that hadn't been funny at all. Colbie hadn't been able to afford college, something she had wanted very much. She had other responsibilities, a mom who wasn't well. Medicine and home care were expensive, even with the state's help. "Oh, here he comes. You *have* to introduce him."

"Sure, but you've got to stop gushing like that."

"He's just so gorgeous. Like an action-film dude."

"Tell me about it." It didn't help that he waded into the store with his wide shoulders braced, his hands fisted and snow clinging to every powerful line. The impression was one of a capable man tested by time and hardship. Hard for a girl like her to resist, a girl who wanted the kind of man she could believe in, one who would never let her down. He definitely looked like that guy.

"If your sister's car is the one with the bike rack, then it has a flat tire. Hand over the keys, and I'll swap it out with the spare. That is, if you have a spare."

"Yes, I do." Leave it to Colbie to walk right up to him with her welcoming smile. She pulled her keys out of her trouser's pocket. "Brianna and I would be deeply indebted to you. If you hadn't noticed, we would have been stranded when we went to leave. At night. In the snow."

"No problem." Max didn't smile but he did take the keys.

When he glanced up, his gaze focused on Brianna with startling impact. The connection returned, although they hadn't touched. A forceful jolt of emotion left her trembling. Time froze. She felt stripped away of her defenses, of all protection. Utterly vulnerable, as if he could see right into her. No one had ever been so close to her before. Panic unfurled within her and she dropped a sugar packet, distantly aware that it was spilling.

"I'll be back." Max turned his back, strode

to the door and called over his shoulder. "I'm counting to three, kid. You had better come help me. Or else."

His wink belied his words as the bells overhead jingled joyfully.

Chapter Six

"I think she really likes you."

Marcus's declaration startled him. What did a kid know about it? Mad, he whipped around to get a good look at the boy, and pain cracked across his skull. How had he forgotten he was halfway under a car?

Just went to show how far gone he was over the woman.

"That had to hurt, bro." Marcus sympathized. "I've never seen you hit your head before. You must really like her, too."

"Mind your own business, Romeo." What did a man have to do for a little privacy? He rubbed the bruise forming on his noggin—good thing he had a hard head—and gave the chains another check. Yep, good and tight. That ought to see the women home safely. This time he crawled out from beneath the car before he lifted his head. "Make yourself useful and take those keys to the ladies."

"Don't you want to do it?"

There was a loaded question. Yes, he did. He would give just about anything to see Brianna again. But looking would lead to talking and talking to liking her even more. What good would come from that?

He wasn't that guy—the one she was looking for. One thing *was* for sure. Whoever that dude turned out to be, the one who won her heart one day, he would be one blessed guy. Max swept the snow off his clothes, for all the good it did. He was wet through from being belly down in the snow. So was his wallet. He handed a snow-speckled twenty to the kid. "Go on. I'm right behind you."

"Sweet." Marcus snatched the greenback and jammed it into his pocket. He took off at a good clip.

"I want the change back!" It didn't hurt to keep the kid on his toes. Max shook his head, and made sure the economy sedan's trunk was closed up tight. Might as well rack up the bike while he was standing here. It would give him something to do instead of stand around in the snow, trying to avoid going back in that store.

Brianna McKaslin. He couldn't stop thinking about her as he hiked her bike into place and tied it down with the chain and lock. The bike had seen better days about a decade ago. Something told him she wasn't a woman who'd had a lot of good breaks in her life.

He didn't like what he'd felt when he'd seen her in the store, snow twinkling in her hair like a tiara, looking wind-blown and wholesome and vulnerable all at once. He felt the same way now, overwhelmed with a steely need to take care of her. To be the one she turned to. To be the man who would keep her safe and happy.

You're not that guy, Max. He would remind himself of it as many times as it took to sink in. He'd learned the hard way as much as a man might want to be a different kind of guy, he could only wind up being himself in the end. Thinking of the past made him wince. Just went to show how much a woman's love—and loss of that love—could affect a man a decade later.

"Max? I thought I was going to do that." Brianna's voice rose above the storm like a gentle melody. She appeared through the curtain of snow with a covered cup in hand. "This will warm you up. You look like you've been laying down in the snow."

"I hope your sister doesn't mind that I put the chains on. I spotted the box in the trunk when I got out the jack and the spare. The roads are going to be tough going. The snow plows aren't out yet." He took the cup she offered, noticing steam rising up through the drink spout. His hands were too numb to feel any of its heat. "Are you two going to be heading out soon?"

"Colbie's closing the store early. She's the assistant manager, so she can make the call. She's the only employee here tonight anyway."

"She won't get any customers in this weather."

"Exactly, which means I don't have to sit around waiting for her to close up, thereby tempting to break my book-budget money."

This is where the guy says, what are you doing on Friday? Want to go out and grab a bite? Max shifted his weight from one foot to the next. Awkward, that's what this was, the moment when you realized you couldn't ask that question. And you suspected she might be waiting for you to.

Just doing you a favor, pretty lady. He gestured toward the building. "You strike me as a budgeting type."

"And what does that mean? Obsessive-compulsive?" She laughed, a musical sound that drove the cold from the snow and the mean from the wind. "You would be right."

"No, no." He noticed a spot of ice outside the back door, where she was heading, so he put his free hand on her shoulder, just to steady her. Just in case. And if a trickle of tenderness lit up the depths of his sorry soul, well, that was something he was just going to have to ignore. Completely. "You're the neat type, aren't you? Everything in its place. Every check recorded in the check register."

"Nothing wrong with being tidy. I like to keep track of things. And it has nothing to do with trying to control my environment."

"'Course not." He could joke, too. It was easier that way. He did it with his brother all the time. Safer to bark and bite and not mean it, than to say what he did mean. He wasn't comfortable with that. He wasn't good at it.

He saw the moment her boot slipped on the ice, she lost her balance and dismay crossed her face. He gripped her harder, holding her upright. Two more steps and they were safely past the ice and beneath the spill of light over the back door.

"You did that and didn't even spill your tea. I'm impressed." She swiped snow from her face with a gloved hand, revealing the luminous emotion in her gorgeous violet eyes. "And I'm grateful."

"No problem." He searched his mind for another quip, something light and funny, something to keep her at a distance. But his brain froze and words failed him. She was small, a petite slip of a woman dressed in blue. The way she gazed up at him, with caring, made him feel ten feet tall. Made him want to reach out and caress the snow from her rosebud mouth. Made him wonder if a kiss from her would be as sweet as the sugary snow gracing her.

As if she realized it, too, her gaze deepened, as if her guards went down again. Vulnerable, he could feel the first notch of her heart falling.

And his.

"Guess we'd better go in." He shook himself back to awareness, back to himself, and pulled open the back door for her. If he was disappointed, he didn't register it. But he did feel hers, a fall of rejection that darkened her eyes and closed her up like a bank vault.

That, he felt. Regret weighed down his steps as he watched her head bow down, presumably against the gusting wind, but maybe also to keep him from reading more of the emotions on her face. He'd let her down. He'd made sure he didn't have a chance with her.

I'm saving you a lot of grief, Beautiful. He followed her into the warmth and when the door slammed shut behind him, it might as well have been the door to his heart. He didn't know what he was thinking, starting to fall for the fairy-tale princess. She just might be for real, but he wasn't going to stick around and find out. Look at her, sugar-sweet and one hundred percent wrong for him.

And, he hated to admit, one hundred percent the kind of woman he would trade his life for.

That didn't mean that he was right for her. He knew a lost cause when he saw it. She might be looking at him with stars in her eyes, but that was because she didn't know him. She didn't know what a failure he was when he came to relationships. He was more like his dad than he wanted to admit. Than he wanted her—a woman he could fall in love with—to know. A woman like Brianna wanted something he knew he didn't have to give. Best to walk away while they were both still whole.

It wasn't what he wanted to do.

He followed her beyond an employee lunch room and down a short hall to the back of the store. The security lights were on, the shelves silent. Only the hush of the heater moving through the vents overhead drew his attention away from the gentle pad of her gait on the industrial carpet. He fought to keep his gaze from trailing after her like his heart wanted to do.

"It's not fair," she said as the cash register and front counter came into sight. "You have to go back out in that cold and put chains on your truck."

"I've got four-wheel drive, so I might not need to. But if I do, the kid will put 'em on. It'll be good for him. Build character."

"I heard that." Marcus stuffed the change back from the twenty into his pocket. "I've got enough character, if you ask me. But you could use some more, old man."

"Thanks for pointing that out." He was twenty-nine to her twenty-two, but those seven years felt like miles. "Where did my change go?"

"I'm keeping it safe for you." The teenager took his purchase from Colbie with a wink and a grin. He loped toward the door. "Guess I'm ready to blow this joint. See you chicks later."

"Bye, Marcus." She kept to the shadows near the shelves. The door jangled closed. "Thanks for everything, Max. I'm glad you took mercy on me and offered to help me out. That's twice now."

"It's my duty to rescue pretty ladies, whether they are in distress or not." He quipped again, the cup of tea still in hand, snow flocking him. "You two be safe driving home. I hope you don't have far to go."

"Not too far." She felt his retreat although he hadn't moved a muscle. Remembering how he had gazed at her for a moment outside, it was as if he were interested in her. But he had turned away. She had the same feeling now. It didn't surprise her. She had reasons why he wasn't the right man for her. He probably had a similar list. It simply wasn't meant to be.

That's a dream for you, she thought as Max opened the door, letting in a current of snow. They aren't substantial. They melt like snow to sunshine. At least that's what she told herself.

"Goodbye, Brianna." Max's gaze held hers for a heartbeat, waiting as if he had something to say. But maybe that was her imagination as he turned and disappeared into the storm and the night.

"He sure was nice." Colbie circled around the edge of the counter with a bank deposit bag. "I can't believe he put chains on my car and changed the tire for me. He's a keeper."

"True, but he's not my keeper." She could tell herself that dreams didn't come true for girls like her, girls who had grown up on the wrong side of the tracks, without love and even less hope. But she would rather believe that, because the truth was harder to face.

She waited while Colbie locked the front doors and shut off the last of the lights, leaving the security ones on to light their way to the back.

"Bree, are you all right?" Colbie looked concerned, the half light accenting her tall, lean frame as she hesitated beside the alarm console. "You look so sad."

"I'm just tired." That was the truth she could admit to. It had been a long day. But her heart and her worries were off-limits. It was easier holding her hurt inside, because she wasn't the only one with problems.

"Colbie, did you need help tonight? I got most of my studying done in the library between classes." She held the back door open, waiting while her sister punched in a few numbers. The alarm began to beep.

"You just said you were tired." Colbie followed her out the door and made sure the lock caught. "You have enough on your mind. Don't you have to meet with the attorney people this week?"

"It's nothing." Or at least, nothing she wanted to burden Colbie with. "You're going out of your way to drive me home. Let me help you."

"Well, you could keep Mom company so I could get some housecleaning done."

"I would be happy to." The storm might be battering her, and the night felt forlorn with spring so far away, but she had faith and she knew what was important. And if her thoughts drifted to Max and how chivalrous he'd looked in the snow, it wasn't only sadness she felt.

She had no experience crushing on someone like that. She hadn't realized before how frightening it was to look a dream in the face. To realize how much it could change your life, and how much it could demand of you.

Glad her heart was covered and safe, and her vulnerability buried, she climbed into the freezing car and dug around for the extra ice scraper. She wasn't going to let her sister do all the work.

"You like her, too. Don't you?" Marcus seemed pretty pleased with himself on that observation.

"No comment." Max killed the engine and yanked the keys from the ignition. The drive home had been dicey, but he was getting used to driving in snow after a winter in Montana. He wondered about the girls, though. No doubt they made it home safely. They didn't have far to go and plenty of experience driving in the white stuff—more than he had—but still. Wondering about Brianna seemed as if it would be a permanent situation for him. "Get inside and tackle your homework. You hear me?"

"Yeah, yeah." Marcus popped out of the passenger seat, making as much noise as an entire basketball team. He grabbed his gear from the back, humming under his breath to the iPod in his pocket, as he went. He slammed the door.

"I still think you should call her. Not many chicks would want to go out with you."

"Stop with the chicks thing. Respect, kid." He unlocked the door. "What are you listening to these days? Maybe you'd better hand over that music player."

"It's just praise music, bro." He swung a duffel bag over one shoulder and a backpack over the other. "Besides, you couldn't figure out how to work my tunes."

"I know, I'm not good at computer stuff." Not that he couldn't find his way around one, but he wasn't a genius at it, the way Marcus was. He marched into the town house, snapping on lights as he went. "Speaking of which, get right to studying. No goofing off. You've done enough of it tonight."

"See? This is why you don't have a wife. Right there." Marcus winked at him. "You're too type A, bro. You've got to chill. Go with the flow. Relax a little. I know just how you can do it."

"Trust me, I don't want to chill." Max shrugged out of his coat and hung it over the back of a kitchen chair to dry. He upped the thermostat and the heater clicked on. "The last time I relaxed, I caught a bullet. Not interested in doing that again."

"It's your life." The kid shook his head, seventeen going on forty. "But you need to think about the choices you're making right now. They can affect you for years to come."

"Yeah, yeah, smarty. One more time. Hit the books."

"Aye, aye, Captain." Marcus's grin was quick and good-natured. "I had a blast today in biochem. Learned some real neat stuff. I can't wait to get a crack at the homework. But while I'm working, I want you to think about what I've said."

Kids. Max shook his head. They think they know everything. He went to the sink and stared down at the pile of dishes, left over from breakfast. He hit the faucet, waiting for the water to warm. Remembering himself about that age—a few years older—and a new recruit, made him cringe. He'd made some choices back then that had changed everything. Made him into the man he was, too hard to believe in anything that wasn't real; too jaded for a certain kind of woman.

Brianna's image flashed in his mind as he rinsed off plates and stacked them in the dishwasher. The silken gold of her hair, the soft curve of her face, the gentle sparkle of her being. He grimaced, fighting a spark of tenderness. But it leaped to life within him, a small stubborn flame that would not extinguish.

A chair scraped across the floor, followed by

a thud as books hit the kitchen table. Marcus, humming away to his hip-hop praise music bebopped to the fridge, hauled out a soda and a handful of cheese slices and dropped into a chair. His books flipped open, his head bent and he hauled out his pencil case with more noise.

See? This is why you don't have a wife. Marcus's words came back to him. *You're too type A, bro. You've got to chill. Relax a little.*

If only that was the real problem. He dropped a handful of flatware into the basket with a clink and clatter. The real problem happened ten years ago. The day he learned to stop trusting everyone. He'd never gotten over the betrayal, or forgiven his own, blind gullibility. Lying in the dark driveway with a cool rain on his face, knowing he was bleeding fast, unable to move, had changed him. It was the reason he hadn't been able to trust in a woman since. He was alone because of it now. He'd turned away from Brianna because of it. Why every date a buddy talked him into going on was doomed. He was no longer that young man. Never would be again.

His cell rang, and he shut off the water. Dried his hands on the front of his shirt before yanking the phone from his pocket. One glance at the screen told him it was trouble. "Dobbs. What are you calling me for?"

"Buddy. Wanted to run something by you." He sounded way too friendly. "Her name is Natalie and she works with my wife. Now, I've never met her, but according to Connie, Natalie has a great personality."

"No way, man. Thanks, but no."

"Now, don't be so quick. She's a CPA, a workaholic kind of lady. You have that in common right there. She might be the one. You don't know until you—"

"No."

"—meet her."

"No." He upended the bottle of detergent and gave it a good squeeze. "I'm not going to let you talk me into this. I don't want to have to pretend I'm interested in small talk." Or in putting my heart on the line, he didn't say. I'm not looking for happily-ever-after.

So why did Brianna's beautiful face flash into his mind?

"Hey, just because Alice didn't work out is no reason why this blind date won't. Give it a shot, Decker. What do you have to lose?"

"My dignity? My pride?" My heart? All of that was already on the line anyway. All it took was one thought of Brianna on her bike at the intersection, dappled with snow and he was precariously close to toppling right off the line of resistance he'd drawn. "I appreciate it, Dobbs, but this isn't the right time."

"All right, but Natalie might not keep. She's the kind a man marries."

So was Brianna.

You've got to stop thinking about Brianna, man. He rammed the dishwasher door shut and punched the wash button. The contraption erupted to life, humming and splashing. He stowed the detergent bottle under the sink. "I'll see you tomorrow at the shop, Dobbs."

He flipped the phone shut to find Marcus staring at him from the other side of the counter. A knowing look was on the kid's face. How could he hear anything over his music?

Apparently he had. He shoved a blue flyer onto the breakfast bar. "Bro, you need to do this."

"Do what?" Max watched the kid head back to his books, the piece of paper bright beneath the track lighting. He grabbed for it and took a look.

"Singles Night at Corner Christian Books." He stared at the heading and frowned. "I'm not going to this."

"Trust me, dude. You need to go. I can't be looking out for you forever. I've got college to think about. I'll be gone, and then you'll be sitting around here by yourself, getting even more bitter."

"Ha-ha. You're funny, kid. I'm not going."

"Too bad, because I am. And you're my ride." Pleased with himself, Marcus gave a Cheshire cat grin before turning back to his biochemistry text.

How about that? The kid was conspiring against him. Before he could argue, his phone rang again. It was work this time. Duty was calling. He grabbed his coat and his keys, feeling every piece of darkness within him and all of the shadows.

"I'll be keeping you in prayer, dear Brianna," Lil, Colbie's mom, trilled from the car's front passenger seat, hands clasped as if already doing so. "I hate that you have to go to trial. It has to break your heart to talk about what happened again. Those lawyer types are putting you through this. It's not right."

"I have a meeting with the assistant district attorney again this Friday." Bree leaned against the backseat, glad for the darkness as Colbie drove through snowy streets toward home. "The trial will be over soon enough and then I never have to remember that night again."

"God willing, you can move on with your life for good." Illness had made Lil frail, and her voice warbled delicately. But the disease could not take her loving nature. "You always have me to talk to, sweet girl. I know you can't turn to your mother."

"Thanks. You know how much you mean to me."

"Not nearly as much as you girls mean to me. I haven't seen Brandi lately. I suppose school and work are keeping her busy." The darkness could not hide the wistfulness in the older woman's tone. "I remember being your age. My days filled with friends and work and getting married. What an exciting time that was. I hope you girls are taking time to have a little fun, too. You all work so hard."

"I had fun tonight." Brianna feared the conversation was going to turn toward dating and marriage prospects, so she made sure to change the direction of the conversation. "I haven't had such a fun evening in forever. My sides still hurt."

"As glad as I was to have you, I can't imagine watching TV reruns with an old woman could have been fun for you. If it was, then I'm very worried about you, Brianna. You are living too solemn of a life!"

"Colbie, help," Brianna joked. "Did you hear what your mom just said?"

"I did. I'm in total agreement with her. You are too serious."

"Me? I laugh all the time. You heard me

tonight. No one's funnier than Laverne and Shirley."

"You're in a rut, girl. School and studying, work and church. The only consistent thing you do for fun is read." Colbie risked a quick glance at her in the rearview mirror. Hard not to see the concern dark in her eyes, although her voice was lightness itself. "You need a change, that's why I'm taking charge of your social calendar again."

"Not again."

"Trust me, it's for your own good. You'll thank me for it later. Don't you think I'm right, Mom?"

"Yes, I certainly do," Lil agreed with a brilliant smile. "It's understandable that you turn inward after something so traumatic. I struggled the same way when I first got my diagnosis, but no matter what, you can't stop living your life. You can't let anything stand in the way of loving this time on earth God has given you."

That's why she was fighting so hard against her fears. Why she was trying to keep her heart open and reach for the good. Hadn't she decided to turn over a new leaf? Replace the fears and the doubts with realistic but positive thoughts? She wanted stability in her life and happiness.

So why did her thoughts turn to Max? Maybe

happy endings weren't meant for girls like her. Look at Colbie's mom. She was as nice as could be, but her life hadn't turned out the way she'd planned. Neither had her own mother's life. Again, memory swooshed through her, taking her back to the snow falling through the security lights behind the back of the bookstore. Of the man standing over her like righteousness and honor, and how his gaze had lingered on her face like a caring touch. How her pulse had skidded to a halt when he'd moved his gaze lower and focused, as if debating a kiss. He had chosen not to take that step.

Maybe that was her answer. One she had to accept.

It doesn't have to mean I can't escape my past and what's happened to me, right, Lord? I have to believe I can. She bowed her head, but the little girl she'd once been, who played make-believe games of being a princess, of finding a happy ending, kept fighting. Kept believing. *Help me, Father. Please show me a better way.*

There was no answer as the windshield wipers beat away the dizzying snow, and the heater blasted lukewarm air into the car. She thought of her devotional tucked inside her backpack, and of the day's verse. *The eternal*

God is your refuge, and his everlasting arms are under you.

"Keep Friday night free," Colbie instructed as she turned into the snowy driveway and stopped the car. "No arguments."

"Why not?" It wasn't as if she was doing anything anyway. "No blind dates."

"It's a group thing, so don't worry." Mischief sparkled in Colbie's smile as she said goodnight.

Colbie was a woman of her word, so Brianna didn't expect the worst as she climbed out into the bitter cold. But she didn't expect the best, either. The night grasped at her like claws as she said her goodbyes, waving as the car backed out into the deep snow, spun a little and then crept away, Lil and Colbie waving in the faint dash lights.

It was as if the dark held all her fears, the ones she had lived through and the ones she had not. Trying to be the girl she'd once been, she trudged to the front steps, trying to keep her fears at bay and tight hold of her faith.

Chapter Seven

Bree was still trembling as she brought her sister's truck to a stop in the bookstore's parking lot Friday evening. The assistant district attorney was a kind woman, capable and understanding. But having to think about the past and about the trial to come chipped away at what hard-won steadiness she had. Wednesday night's snow was nothing more than a few splotches in shady places, replaced by a drizzly rain that made it feel as if winter was thinking twice about making another comeback.

She yanked the keys out of the ignition as her cell buzzed. A text message. Probably one of her sisters checking up on her, bless them. She really could use sisterly support about now when the echoes of that night, the gunshots and the terror, seemed to whisper in the rain.

How R U? U R in my prayers. Luv, B.

Brooke. With all of her problems, she had taken the time to remember about today's meeting. That meant a lot. She tapped back a message.

I'm OK, thanx. Keeping U in my prayers 2. Luv, Bree.

She hit Send, wondering how her half sister was and if Brooke would ever come back to Montana for good, when a slam shattered the stillness. Her heart dropped six inches. Her palms went clammy. Adrenaline spilled into her blood. She stiffened, staring through the water-streaked windshield, as if danger was close.

You're fine, Bree. She spotted someone walking away from their vehicle, striding through the rain toward the brightly lit book-store. See? It was just someone slamming their door. Not a gunshot.

But the stress lingered, and she blinked hard against the flashback chasing her. The sound was a trigger that sent her back to that night. To the hard burn of the tile floor against her knees, the realization that Juanita was not re-sponding to CPR, and the torquing pain as the gunman grabbed her by the arm.

It's over now, Bree. It's just a memory. You're

safe now. She gathered her purse, and with her phone clutched in one hand, she clattered out of the car, realizing too late that she'd forgotten to unbuckle. Her fingers fumbled with the seat belt, and she felt like an idiot.

If Colbie looked out the window and saw her right now, she would come running in concern, and there was no way she wanted to worry her sister like that. Bree untangled herself, digging deep for composure. Colbie had enough on her plate. Besides, she was fine. See? She was standing on her own two feet, safe and sound and perfectly okay.

And if the remembered echoes of the gunmen's violent screaming remained, she didn't have to listen to it. If the helplessness she'd felt continued to claw at her, she could ignore that, too. Cool water tapped over her, and she let the sound of the rain wash away the noise of the past. She drew her spine straight, chin up, grappling for every bit of inner strength she had. What had her therapist said? The only way out of hardship and pain was to go straight through it.

Well, she was strong enough. She was not helpless anymore.

She hadn't taken two steps when the back of her neck tingled beneath the warmth of her scarf. This time it wasn't old fears that made her nervous system jump into high gear and her neurons misfire. Her fingers lost contact with her bag, and it tumbled to her feet with a wet plop. Her knees weakened as she heard the distinct knell of a man's confident steps coming up behind her. A gait she somehow recognized. Her senses sharpened, as if eager to see the man's handsome face and hear the cozy warmth of his baritone.

"I noticed you were having a few problems. Are you all right now?" Max Decker knelt to retrieve her handbag. In a black raincoat and a black sweater, jeans and hiking boots, he could have walked right out of her daydreams.

Not that he belonged in her dreams. She did her best not to remember the last night they had been together, and the hope she'd felt. The hope his brother had figured out. The kiss that didn't happen. Awkward, sure, but did she want him to know that? Never. Nada. No way.

"You probably need this." He straightened to his full six-feet-plus height and held out her bag.

No grin. Just his hard features and his un-blinking gaze. Was he remembering that night in the snow, too?

"Yes. Thanks." Brilliant, Bree. Way to impress him with your witty banter. Way to show him she wasn't feeling uncomfortable at all. "I didn't expect, I mean—What are you doing here?"

"That's what I was about to ask you." His startling blue eyes fastened onto hers. "The kid talked me into coming to Singles Night. He was hoping to meet some babes."

"Babes?" Why was she laughing?

"He was just trying to get a reaction from me. And I'm pretty sure he's going to get it." Max jammed his hands into his jacket pockets, strolling easily through the rain. "I think my brother and your sister have been conspiring."

"Uh?" Great. Now her brain was malfunctioning, too. "You don't mean they tried to set us up?"

"That's exactly what I mean. Marcus!" Max turned around, shouting through the rain.

A few rows back, a door shut and a tall kid emerged from the shadows. "You called, Captain?"

"He thinks he's being funny. That is out of one of those star voyage trek shows he watches. You probably don't know how it is. I'm sure you and your sisters get along just great."

"Now why would you assume that?"

"Just look at the lot of you. Wholesome and sweet. I haven't seen so much niceness outside of a Christmas movie in my entire life." He smiled, although his features still looked rough and stony, and she didn't know how to take his words. She didn't have to think of anything to say, because he kept on talking to his brother. "I've figured out what you did. You ought to come apologize to Brianna. It's an insult to her, trying to fix her up with a guy like me."

"True," Marcus agreed with a good-natured chuckle. "I never thought of it that way. Sorry, Bree."

"I'll find a way to forgive you."

"I was told there are a lot of pretty high school girls who come over from the church down the street." Marcus sauntered by, looking tidy and wrinkle-free with every hair in place. "I'm looking for a girlfriend. Unlike my brother, I'm not a lone wolf."

"Funny." He held open the door, first for the kid strolling through with enough confidence for three men, and then for Brianna. Seeing her again felt like he'd taken a sucker punch. He felt disoriented, like coming inside too fast after being out in bright sunlight. Blinded, he waited while Brianna swept away past him, smelling of lilacs and spring rain.

The store was warm and busy, full of people sipping hot drinks and nibbling on cookies. Piano music piped in over the speakers accompanied the low roar of conversation. He picked out Colbie in the crowd, who was tall and slender, talking to a foursome of high school girls, about the kid's age.

"Gotta go charm the ladies." Marcus winked, so sure of himself, as he sauntered away. "Adios."

"Bye, Marcus." Bree's melodic voice warmed with humor. "Anyone can see you've done a great job with him. I didn't ask. Are you raising him on your own, or is his mom nearby, too?"

"No, Jean stayed in California. I'm solely responsible for the boy, for better or worse." Max winced as the kid strolled up to Colbie and the knot of girls like he was a movie star. "That boy has self-confidence in spades. I don't know where he gets it."

"I can't imagine." Her tone was both wry and light at the same time.

It was tempting to want to look at her, to take in her beauty and her light, to let the inevitable happen. But he held back. He knew better. When he wanted to banter, maybe add some self-deprecating humor, he took a step away from her and focused his eyes on his brother—not on Brianna.

He cleared his throat, just in case any of that wish would be a hint in his voice. "I'm going to blow this joint. Got things to do."

Dry cleaning to drop off. Bills to mail at the post office. A few groceries to pick up. But she didn't need to know the mundane details. Best not to let this be personal, not anymore.

"Oh. Aren't you going to stay?"

He strained to pick up any disappointment in her words, but he couldn't be sure. When he grabbed hold of the door, he denied he was feeling any form of that same emotion. "As Marcus said, I'm his ride. How long will this shindig last?"

"Probably a couple hours."

Time to go. He wasn't going to stand around and watch her talk with any of the guys in the room. There were quite a few of them, neat and well-dressed young men, who looked polite and proper and well versed in which forks to use at the dinner table. He stared hard at the doorframe and not at her. "Enjoy."

"It's a possibility. I don't see any dudes with a nose ring or a Mohawk. It's more promising than the last time Colbie tried to set me up."

"Then I wish you luck." He instructed his feet to move, but they stayed rooted to the floor. To be honest, he didn't want to leave. He wouldn't mind spending the next few hours or so talking with Bree, basking in the glow of her gentle smile and giving in to the need to care about her even more.

But he felt every one of his twenty-nine years. Every shadow of his experience. Every mile of the road he had walked. He spent his days on the dark side of life, and that had changed him. He would never be one of those fresh-faced guys wearing a shirt and tie, who saw life as an easier, friendlier place. Men like those over there by the book display had time and a whole heart to give to a lady.

All he had was a battered and bruised soul. She deserved better. Even if the thought of her gazing up at one of those guys with her earnest violet eyes and sweet smile made him want to put his hand through the glass. Not that he would, of course. It took all his self-control to face her. To do this the right way. "See you around, Brianna."

"You don't want a cookie before you leave?"

"In case you haven't noticed, I'm not a cookie kind of guy."

"I'm not sure what a cookie kind of guy is."

"Try over there." He gestured with a single nod at the crowd of single men talking near the devotionals display before he pulled open the door.

A pair of women were on their way in, and he held the door for them. The newcomers made it impossible to say more. She waited. The damp and cold blew in, and she shivered.

"Maybe Colbie got it right this time," he said as he backed through the door.

"Maybe." She wrapped her arms around her

middle, cold from the blast of the wind and from something else. "Drive safe in that storm."

"Sure." That was his last word to her as his boot hit the sidewalk and he let the door close. She thought she saw a look of regret in his dream-blue eyes, but she couldn't be sure. He took the final step that launched him out of the light's reach and he became a shadow and then nothing at all.

"He's not staying?" A hand landed on her shoulder, a comforting touch. Colbie joined her at the window, trying to catch sight of the man in the downpour.

"No. He said he had things to do."

"You sound a little sad about that. Do you like him?"

She jerked inside at the personal question. Equal parts of panic and sorrow filled her. "What's not to like?"

"Exactly." Colbie's grip tightened comfortingly. "He likes you."

"I don't think so." Why else would he walk away. Again? "It's probably for the best. He makes me panic."

"Panic? As in you're afraid of him?"

"Not of him." She swallowed, feeling sorely alone as she stared out into the night. A set of red taillights glinted faintly through the dark.

Max's truck? Probably. "I didn't know how hard it was to almost get what you want."

"I'm not following you." Colbie's words were kind and sympathetic, although she didn't understand.

How could she? Bree didn't understand it herself. "When I'm with him, it's like standing on the top of the tallest mountain in the world, without a parka to keep me warm or a rope to anchor me, and feeling the glacier I'm standing on begin to crack. It's a long way to fall."

"It's a lot to live up to."

"Exactly." And she left unsaid the other fears. Of not being enough. Of being so vulnerable. Of being so close to someone. Of losing what matters most. "I'm starting to rethink my decision to find Mr. Perfect. It's a rocky, perilous road."

"Amen, sister."

Did Colbie have those same fears? It didn't make her feel any less alone. "I need some carbs. That's bound to cheer me up."

"Come with me. I brought Mom with me tonight. I know she'd like to talk with you." Colbie took her by the hand, and they headed to the cookie table together.

All through his errands, Max had been frustrated with himself. How come doing the right thing didn't feel that way? He'd groused about it as he tossed a head of iceberg lettuce into a bag and went on to grab a bag of carrots. By the time he stood in line at the checkout, he had almost been good with it. Even he would have matched up dear, sweet Brianna with one of those fresh-faced, clean-cut types. Nothing to be unhappy about, right?

The line moved up, and he angled the cart to the stand and began unloading. The checker chatted with the customer ahead of him, making small talk as he dumped a half dozen cans of chili onto the belt. He was good with his life as it was, right? He liked being a lone wolf. Thanks to the lessons he had learned from Nancy, it was better that way. Safer.

But as he loaded a six-pack of cola next to the chili, he realized something had changed. He couldn't put his thumb on what. He kept unloading vegetables, deli meat, chips and a loaf of bread, working quick and efficiently. His thoughts kept returning to Brianna, looking upset as she'd wrestled with her seat belt and how she had stumbled out of the car. How she had looked so lovely in the rain.

The conveyer belt chugged his stuff up to the cashier, who smiled at him. "Did you find everything you were looking for?"

He nodded once, but he couldn't say that he

had. Brianna's image stuck with him, vulnerable and petite and fragile-looking. If he hadn't known about what she'd been through, he would never have guessed her strength or the magnitude of her valor. He couldn't say he didn't admire her for that.

Fine, maybe he *more* than admired her.

The drive through the evening streets proved uneventful. Rain hammered the vehicle with enough force, the wipers couldn't keep up. Water levels grew on the roads and ran in streams along the curb. The traffic was light, and he pulled into the bookstore's lot in record time.

Did he go in? He sat in the truck, the engine idling, the defroster battling the fog at the rim of the windshield. The world was night shadows and rain, shades of black and gray. Maybe that's why his gaze was attracted to the lemony light behind the store's glass windows and the splashes of color from the book displays and the people as they sat in folding chairs, lined up listening to a blond lady talk to the group. Someone raised their hand—looked like a question-and-answer session of some kind—and the blond lady answered with a pleasant smile. It was all very nice, sure. But it wasn't why his gaze was drawn to the bright lights and honey colors and the tranquil scene.

No. It was a certain woman he searched for. Her particular shade of perfect gold hair. Her darling face he longed to see.

This is not like you, Max. He shook his head, unhappy with himself even as he searched for her through the rain-streaked glass. When he found her on the far side of the crowd, she wasn't seated like everyone else. No, Brianna knelt at the side of an older woman in a wheelchair, her face upturned, filled with love.

His battered, sorry heart turned over and thumped to life one painful beat followed by another. Feelings he'd thought had died long ago flooded his chest, leaving him helpless and drowning.

You've got to stop this now, man. He shut off the engine and yanked the keys from the ignition, the rounding drum of the rain on the roof the only sound. Somehow he had to figure how to stuff those feelings back inside where they'd been hiding. He was not a guy run by emotions. He was methodical and logical. That's what made him a good detective, and a prudent man.

When he climbed out of the truck, he concentrated on the cold slap of rain against his face and the splash of his boots in the puddled lot. If his gaze didn't stray from her, then he didn't worry about it. He was in control of his emotions, in control of his heart.

If it seemed to him that she was the most beautiful girl in the room, then it was only a fact, not his feelings taking over. If the light seemed to follow her, and the gold in her hair gleamed like platinum, then it wasn't because he was sweet on her. Her beauty was a fact, like the storm and the concrete curb he was stepping over. Verifiable facts, which anyone could agree on. The fact that he could not force his gaze from her was immaterial.

She drew him through the darkness and into the light, from the cold of the storm into the store's sheltering warmth. Rain sluiced down his face, and he swiped it away. The pleasant noise of conversations, the people, the fragrance of brewing coffee and spiced cider faded into nothing. All he could see was Brianna, folding her skirt as she slipped into a chair beside the older woman. All he could hear was the low tones of Brianna's voice, as the speaker relinquished the floor. All he could sense was her startled gaze as she glanced over her shoulder to see him.

Her reaction came purely, simply. Her eyes lit with subtle fondness, and when a smile touched her soft lips, it was like a new beginning.

He couldn't deny it any longer. He wasn't the same man. He had changed, and it was because of her.

Chapter Eight

Brianna rose on shaky knees. Max was back. She was up on that mountain again, feeling the glacier crack beneath her feet. She laid a hand on Lil's arm. "I'm going to get some tea. Do you want a refill?"

"No, I'm fine, dear. You go on."

Somehow she circled around the wheelchair and the rows of emptying chairs. She was halfway to the beverage table before she realized it. The reason: Max strode toward her, sucking all the air in the room and the cells from her brain as he approached.

She couldn't breathe. She couldn't speak. All she could see was him drawing nearer, his boots eating up the distance until suddenly he towered over her. Her skin prickled as if lightning was about to strike. She felt vulnerable, down to the quick, down to the soul. How could a man have such an emotional impact on her? It was as if he were a force field, and being near him disabled her defensive shields.

"Let me." He took the cup from her grip, commanding and shy all at once. "I saw you weren't alone."

"No, I certainly wasn't. With Lil, it was love at first sight."

"Lil? Is she your mom?" He strode over to the table and grabbed hold of the hot water carafe. Although more distance separated them, he felt closer than ever.

"No, she's Colbie's mom. But I've adopted her."

"I can see why."

Everything around her *seemed* perfectly normal: the steaming tea, the plop of the bag into the water, the faint sound of a romantic piano lilting from the store speakers. She didn't *feel* normal. Not even a little bit. As if suddenly she found herself staring thousands of feet straight down a mountainside and discovering she had a serious fear of heights.

"What about your mom?" she asked, her wobbly hands separating a clean cup off the stack. "Are you close?"

"Sure. She's retired to Palm Springs. She's popular around Christmastime, especially with the weather around here. We keep in touch, mostly e-mail. Has the kid been giving you any trouble tonight?"

"No." She set the cup on the table, waiting for him to pour. She had to steel herself. Max had a habit of walking away. He was just here to get his brother and then he'd be gone, that was all. She had to survive only a few more minutes, and the discomforting sense of terror would be over. "Marcus has been amusing us all evening."

"Yeah, he's good at that. Let me guess." He slipped a protective sleeve on the cup before setting it on the table for her. "He's tried his charms on every teenage girl here and they all rejected him."

"That would be putting it mildly."

"Yeah, the kid thinks he's with-it, but he hasn't found a girlfriend yet. And it's not for lack of trying." He took the empty cup and filled it, too. "He's sadly lacking when it comes to conversing with the ladies. I would help him if I could, but you've seen me in action. And you've heard about my worst date failure."

"True. Poor Marcus. He's about as hopeless as his big brother is."

"That's the truth." He poked through the open boxes and chose a mint tea bag.

"Although I am a little sweet on him. Marcus, I mean." Why did she say that? Worse, she was blushing. If she kept this up, Max was going to guess in about the next two seconds she had a serious crush on him.

"I could tell." He simply shrugged one wide shoulder as he tore open the packet and dunked the bag into the water. "So, did you meet any promising single men?"

There was a telling question. Panic tapped through her veins in a sprightly staccato. "I met a lot of people tonight."

Not a single one of the perfectly nice Christian men could hold a candle to Max.

"Me being here with you right now is wrecking your chances of a decent guy coming over to ask you out." His observation sounded casual as he leaned against the wall, looking like a hero come to life. All he was missing was an Indiana Jones hat and a sidekick.

"You're not a decent guy?"

"I'm not what you're looking for, that's for sure." He took a cautious sip of tea.

"You say that like you know what I'm looking for."

"It's no mystery, Bree. Look at you. You could be Candy Cane Princess at the Christmas parade."

"And that means I'm looking for the Candy Cane Prince?"

"Funny." He didn't laugh but his dark eyes

glinted with amusement. "You need someone normal. Tame. Tie-wearing. The kind of guy who isn't afraid to eat quiche and cry."

"A lot you know about me." She joined him at the wall. The panic could go away any time, thanks, because there was no reason for it. Why wasn't her heart listening? "What about you? There are still lots of nice women here. You could mingle. See if anyone strikes your fancy."

"I'm not really interested in dating." He took another sip of tea, as if that was the end of the topic.

Not a chance, bud. Her curiosity was hooked. "If you're not interested in dating, then why were you out on a blind date?"

"Peer pressure." A wry grin hooked the corner of his mouth.

"I can't see a big strong man like you succumbing to peer pressure."

"I was just trying to fit in. Be like the rest of the guys with their wives and fiancées," he quipped, dimples carving deep. "I struck out, which was just as well. My dating history is abysmal."

"Abysmal is better than practically nonexistent."

"Wait, now you've got to have had a boyfriend before."

"Nope, no boyfriends." Hard to admit. Very

hard. She took a sip of tea and stared at the crowd. Some people were starting to leave. Lil, bless her, was chatting happily to Lucy, the author who had come to speak to the group tonight.

"Not one boyfriend? I don't believe it."

"It's true." Bree felt her insides coil up. She didn't like looking back into the past. "Why do you think I let Colbie set me up on so many blind dates?"

"You mean you've been out on dates, just not anything serious, like with a fiancé."

"No. I have never let any guy get that close." The truth made her feel even more unprotected, as if she were starting to tumble right off the top of that impossibly high mountain with no safety rope to catch her. "My high school years were too chaotic. My dad left, my mom found a new husband and he was mean. The last thing I wanted was to try to trust another guy."

"High school was a long time ago."

"True, but when Brandi and I moved here to Bozeman to attend the university, life became good. Really good." With the way the light shone on her, she looked spotlighted, as if a painter had rendered her that way, the center of someone's world. "We rented our own little place, and suddenly we were settled. None of Mom's meltdowns or all-night arguments. We were stable. Brandi and I were in charge. We could make sure we had a place to live because we paid the rent on time. We had enough food in the house because we had jobs. Our money wasn't always disappearing. We had peaceful evenings and uninterrupted sleep."

"I take it your mom set the bar low when it came to men?"

"Low? If it were any lower, we could have seen the Great Wall of China."

"Understood." He saw what she didn't say. He'd seen it enough as a cop. "Then you've probably raised your bar pretty high to compensate."

"I don't know. When I find someone who can top it, I'll let you know." She blushed, a hint of pink rosying her face.

That was pretty much the answer he was expecting. Chances were, he wouldn't measure up to that high-set bar. So, why didn't that stop him from appreciating her amazing beauty? How she could look radiant in a plain pink sweater and simple tan skirt captivated him. Her loveliness couldn't be found on a magazine's glossy page or enhanced with any amount of makeup. As striking as she was, her true loveliness shone from the inside, like a pearl's luster in perfect light.

"How about you?" She turned those stunning

violet eyes on him. "Why aren't you looking for your soul mate?"

"I don't believe in soul mates. Doesn't exist."

"Of course they do." She looked crestfallen. "Or why else would there be books and movies about it?"

"Hype to part the consumer from their hard-earned dollars."

"I saw that smirk. You're not fooling me, buster. Otherwise, why else would people fall in love and get married?"

"Loneliness, mostly."

"Even you don't believe that."

If anyone could make him believe in the concept of soul mates, then it would be her. Yep, that was a change, too. Steam bathed his face as he took a sip of tea. The minty heat scorched his tongue, taking his mind off what was happening to his heart. "Some days I find the idea of true love more unlikely than on others."

"Are those the days you go out on dates?"

"Funny." He scanned the room, alert. "No, I keep hoping there's someone out there for me, but I'm not sure there is."

"Surely you've tried to find out."

"I did. Once I thought I had found her." His confession rang low, and he hoped none of his emotions from that time were coming through.

He liked to think that was well behind him. "I met Nancy in church."

"In church?" Her forehead crinkled adorably in disbelief.

"You say that like you're surprised. I'm a believer." When she crooked one eyebrow in question, he chuckled. "All right, I believe in God. Just not true love. Anyway, Nancy was one of those innocent types. Pure goodness."

"You fell in love with her."

"I fell hard." He winced, not daring to take a look at the woman by his side. "I fell too hard. I thought she was perfect. My world revolved around that girl."

"That doesn't surprise me." She took a sip of her tea. "I can see that about you."

"Yeah?" That young man didn't exist anymore. The one who could put all his belief in a woman. In anyone. He had loved with every fiber of his being, with every inch of his life. For all the good it had done him. He'd been stupid. He'd been fooled. He'd been gullible, believing in her goodness, one trait that hadn't really existed. He could still taste the bitter wound on his tongue and feel it in his soul. "I actually almost asked her to marry me. Hard to believe that, huh?"

"Not in the slightest." Her tender tone drew his gaze. He fought it, but it did no good. It was as if his spirit turned toward hers, like darkness finding its light. His throat filled right along with his heart. He had never felt so revealed. As if she saw him, the real man he was, the guy behind the tough cop facade and lone-wolf defenses.

Maybe that's why he found himself opening up. The story he'd done his best to forget through the years tumbled out like rocks rolling down a steep hill. "She said I kept her at a distance. I didn't let her in. The job was a big part of it. Constant calls. Constant late nights. Problems that I couldn't let go of at shift's end. I was nineteen years old, wet behind the ears, just out of the academy and still figuring out my way."

"What happened?"

"She betrayed me. She broke my heart into bits. Don't think I ever figured out how to put it back together again."

"I read somewhere once that pain is God's way of growing your heart. That when it heals, it's stronger and better, capable of more love and compassion."

Yeah, he figured she would believe something like that. She wasn't just a storybook princess on the outside, but on the inside, too. She gazed up at him with honesty so pure, he lost his breath.

Careful, he thought, you can't let her get to you like that. Sometimes a man needed to believe in goodness. Sometimes a man saw too much of the bad side of humanity and what people were capable of, and it clung to him like soot. He'd been wrong before. Very wrong. He grimaced, thinking of Nancy. It was his experience that goodness was too fragile to survive long in the real world. That good on this earth wasn't as strong as evil.

"How did she betray you?" Her question was little more than a whisper.

The reaction within him went off like a bomb. "Nancy was good at pretending to be something she wasn't."

"Do you mean, lying?"

"Yep. Not long after we broke up, I came home one night. I was just getting out of my car when I heard footsteps running down the street. It's residential. Quiet kind of neighborhood, so I think, maybe it's teenagers out running around before their parents figure it out. So I wasn't paying any more attention than that. Then I was shot in the back. It was her old boyfriend. You see, when we first started dating, they were broken up, but he didn't let go. Kept stalking her. A couple buddies and I set him straight, told him to leave her alone."

"And he came after you?"

"After she went back to him. What she didn't tell me, was that he was a drug dealer, and she'd had a prior problem with drugs. She hid it well for a while. " He might have thought he was hiding his pain as he shrugged his shoulders, like it was nothing. But he didn't fool her.

"That had to be devastating."

"It was rough, but I got through it."

But not over it. That was easy to see. "At least the man who shot me wasn't anyone I knew. It wasn't personal. I always used to think that made it worse, like the world was more unsafe or something, but it's not true. Betrayal like you went through has to be worse."

"A bullet is a bullet. Bet you didn't think we would have that in common."

"No. I didn't." Unspoken understanding passed between them. The helplessness and fear, the fight to recover and heal. It was a difficult journey. She could see how deeply he had been hurt. He may have recovered physically, but emotionally, a person never was the same after something like that. Some emotional wounds would always scar.

"The thing that got to me the most, was that she had this other life separate from me. She was in contact with him. I guess she saw him frequently toward the end. She kept so many secrets. I didn't see any of it. I thought she was the sweetest woman, and I was wrong. I never want to be that blind again."

"Or to trust anyone so much?"

"True. That doesn't mean I'm not tempted now and then." Dimples chased away the hint of his shadows, making him stronger than ever in her view. "We're a pair. Both of us distrustful. Can't find anyone to date."

"Speak for yourself."

"Uh, need I remind you how we met?" A hint of humor flickered in his perfectly blue eyes. He drained his cup. "I distinctly remember it was one of your date-failure moments."

"Okay, so it *was* doom. That doesn't mean I can't hold out hope that eventually I will have the perfect date with the absolutely right guy."

"Hope is risky. It might work out, or you might be disappointed." Still that smirk and that glint of amusement on his chiseled granite face. "I personally avoid hope of any kind. I'm not a risk-taking guy."

"I won't let go of my hope. Nothing can make me. God said His purpose was to give us hope."

"Yes, He did."

Being this near to him was like being in a gravity vortex. If she was precariously balancing on the edge of a cracking glacier, then he was the gravity ready to grab her feet and pull her down into a ten-thousand-foot free fall. She pushed away from the wall, trying to get distance from him and finished the dregs of tea in her cup. "I have to keep hoping that maybe next time it will be the right guy. The one who will sweep me off my feet and will be my lifelong true love."

"And carry you off to his castle?"

"Well, after the wedding. Sure. I'm a traditional girl." She tossed her empty cup into the garbage can, doing her best not seem as if she wasn't falling down that mountainside. "I suppose you don't believe in true love, either?"

"No, but I wish you luck finding it." He strolled over to her, gravity vortex and all. He tossed the cup into the can. "I hope he comes with a fancy castle and a happily-ever-after just for you."

"I'm not interested in a fancy castle, but I do hope you're right." She thought about her past, her turbulent childhood and the endless string of men parading through her mother's life. She wanted something better. If that were possible. So, why did it feel as if gravity had won, the glacier had crumbled apart and she was falling through midair?

Max is not right for you, Bree. She began to switch off the hot plate for the tea water and the coffee pot, needing something constructive to do. Something real, because she was having an emotional vertigo moment. She'd lost balance, she'd lost perspective, beginning to pine after this amazing man who was wrong for her in every way. Sure, at first glance he had been her dream man come to life. Aside from the fact that he wasn't interested in her, there were plenty of reasons it couldn't work.

She grabbed the stack of unused cups and stuffed them back into the box under the cloth-covered table. Reason number one: too cynical. Reason number two: doesn't believe in true love. Reason number three: being near him is like an emotional free fall. Reason number four: he's everything I want and everything I'm afraid of all at the same time.

"You never told me how it's working out with the car situation." Did he move away? No, he came closer, apparently unaware of the effect he had on her. "Have you received your check yet?"

Her spirit seemed to brighten and lean toward him, another proof of his force-field effect. She stacked up the unused paper napkins, hoping he didn't notice that her fingers kept fumbling. "It came in yesterday's mail, but I'm still car-less. Face it. My car wasn't worth that much, so the check isn't extravagantly high. What can I get for that kind of money? I need a vehicle that is in good condition, but not a breakdown waiting to happen. What are the chances of finding it?"

"So you haven't started looking?"

"Oh, I've looked. Online mostly. I'm not liking what I see. The right thing will come along, I'm sure of it." She wrapped up the napkins and slipped the package into the box. "It's going to take time."

"Your hope is showing."

"Yes, I know." She felt his magnetism; she didn't have to look up to know he was leaning against the wall again, dangerously close, his gaze zeroed in on her like she was a crime he was trying to solve. Great. He was probably thinking she was a negotiating wimp—and he wouldn't be wrong. "I'm praying on it, and I'm sure it will work out."

"Until then you've got your bike, right?"

"Right, when I can't borrow Brandi's truck." Could she resist looking at him?

No, of course not. Mostly because she wanted to see the stretch of his smile, the carve of his dimples and the stalwart, solid look of him, the kind of man who did no wrong, a man who faced his responsibilities, who stood tall for what was right.

Okay, she wasn't just falling for him. She *had* fallen, hard and fast at terminal velocity.

Oops. Why else was she singing his praises? This was a serious disaster in the making. She focused on putting away the paper plates next and concentrating on the task, when all she wanted was to bask in his smile and make him laugh so she could hear the low-throated rumble. Yep, she was in serious trouble.

"If you need car-shopping advice, let me know." Everything about him shouted "casual" as he jammed his hands into his bomber jacket pockets. His tone, his gestures, his face, it was all impartial, as if he were a cop offering a lost driver directions. "I know a few people."

"A few people?" She curled her slender fingers around the back of a wooden chair and peered at him, as if trying to see deep inside him. "Who are you, and just who do you know, Detective Decker?"

"People." He adopted a Jimmy Stewart accent. "Don't you worry about a thing."

Hold on to your heart, Bree. And do it now. If she didn't, she was going to start making a list of all the ways Max *was* right for her. That would only lead to total romantic disaster. She might not be the most worldly girl in the world, but she knew that no way was Max offering to help her because he was falling for her. No, this was purely platonic. A gesture of friendship and because he was that kind of a man. He made a difference. He helped others. He did the right thing.

So, why was she nodding? Why couldn't she hold back the fateful words? "Sure. If you have the time."

"I do. Great. Give me your cell number."

She rattled it off, watching as he punched keys on his phone, adding her to his electronic phone book.

Should she do the same? What had become of her phone? She checked both skirt pockets. Empty. Where was her purse? She must have lost all common sense when Max had strolled into the bookstore because she'd obviously left it somewhere. He dominated her view, and it took effort to turn away from him. She was shocked to realize the store was nearly empty. That Marcus and a few other guys were folding up and stacking the chairs, and Lil was wheeling closer with a bag in her lap—her handbag, thank heavens.

"I hate to interrupt." Lil rolled closer. "It's always nice to see young people getting acquainted."

By getting acquainted, Bree knew what Lil meant. She had a mother's glimmering hope that shone from her like the bold rays around an eclipse. Lil didn't stop there. "I have to confess I was doing a little detective work on my own. I learned from Marcus—what a nice young man—that you and Bree have been out to pizza together. The things I have to learn second hand."

"Did Marcus mention that he was there, too?" Max interjected before she could explain, his easygoing manner and charm flawlessly dazzled as he took Lil's offered hand in his own. "Nice to meet you, ma'am. It's been a long while since I was in the company of so many lovely ladies."

"If you're trying to get on my good side, it's working." The older woman dimpled, pleasure chasing away the lines on her face. "I also hear that you're raising your brother. That kind of commitment to family can be hard to find these days."

"I don't think you can call it commitment." He looked uncomfortable with the praise. He was a modest sort, Bree realized. And that was another thing for her reasons-to-like-Max list that she *wasn't* compiling.

Or at least, trying not to.

"Mostly no one else would take Marcus, so I got stuck. Couldn't help it. It was unavoidable. Now I've grown fond of the kid, so it's hard to get rid of him."

She was *so* not fooled. She could see what Max didn't say, what he was uncomfortable saying. This was a man who had scars, too. Who had learned, just like she had, that it was safer not to let your feelings show. Safer not to let anything or anyone appear to mean too much to you.

"Here's your bag, sweetie." Lil handed it over with a smile. "Now, never mind me, you two. I've got to track down my daughter. I don't know where she's gotten off to. Go back to your talking. Nice to meet you, Max."

"And you, ma'am." He nodded once, perhaps a sign of respect, as Lil rolled her wheelchair in the direction of the checkout counter. "I can see why you've adopted her."

"She's the best." Her phone was right where it belonged, lost in the bottom of her bag. She handed it over.

"I'll send you a text sometime tomorrow. I'll have a bead on a car for you by then." Max didn't bat an eye, there was no hint of his emotion as he punched in his phone number. From the thick dark hair swirling over his strong forehead, to his deep-set eyes and the stoic expression and stubbornly set jaw, he simply made a girl want to sigh.

"Are you sure you're good with this? You've played the shining knight a few times now."

"My armor isn't shining. Never was. It's tarnished and dinged, trust me. But I'd like to help you." Impossible to read the glance of emotion as he pressed the phone into her palm. His touch was callused and a few moments too long, almost as if he didn't want to move away. "Here comes Marcus. I'd better drag him away. It's past his curfew."

"It's nine o'clock."

"Yep. I look forward to seeing you again." Max strolled away, wide shoulders set, back straight, warrior strong.

The pang of emotion in her heart resonated through her, radiating out like waves in a pond as she watched him open the door for his brother. The chimes overhead jingled cheerfully and he stood before the threshold, framed by light. He lifted one hand in a brief wave, his last farewell. Affection deepened his true-blue eyes and zinged through the air between them. Something had changed. Everything had changed.

He strode through the threshold and into the dark, leaving an image in her heart that did not fade.

Chapter Nine

The chimes over the bakery's front door tinkled a merry welcome as the door flew open, bringing with it blustery wind and tenacious sunshine. Brianna turned from her work at the back counter to greet the new customer. It was Colbie, looking fresh and lovely in an olive-green coat, white cable-knit sweater, jeans and suede boots.

"Hey, stranger." She abandoned folding boxes. "Good to see you."

"I love Saturdays. Errands and not having to go to work, although I do love my job." Colbie strode to the counter with a smile and an agenda. "I've got Mom in the car, so I can't be long. How about a half dozen banana muffins? They're her favorite."

"Sure. Do you want to pick out the faces?" Bree donned a plastic glove and grabbed a small bakery box from the stack she'd already made. "I got to decorate the muffins this morning. A total blast."

"Mom will adore the smiling monster. I like the ones with the snaggletooth. How about three of each?"

"You got it." She carefully loaded the box with the enormous muffins sporting iced monster faces. "How's your day off going?"

"Good. We just finished battling the grocery store. Mom wanted to come. She misses doing it herself." Colbie opened her purse and dug through her wallet. She dropped a five-dollar bill on the counter. "She's lost so much of her freedom, I want her to feel like she can still do some things. Like pick out what type of potato chips she wants."

"She looked good at the bookstore last night." Bree moved over to the register and caught sight of Lil in the car, parked at the curb in front of the windows. She waved. Lil waved back, cheerful as always in spite of her infirmity. Bree punched in the sale at the discounted rate the owner, their cousin Ava, insisted on. She knew how hard things were for Colbie and her mom. "It was good to see Lil chatting with everyone. A social butterfly."

"She gets lonely these days. She always was a people person. I'm grateful for our church's home-care circle. Having church members visit on a weekly basis has been a lifesaver for her. She doesn't always feel up to going out."

"I'm going to try to make it by after church tomorrow." Brianna counted back the change. "I need to study, but at least you can get out for a while."

"I'd appreciate it. I'll probably tackle the yard work. The leaves are still in the yard from last October. It's scary, that's what it is." Colbie took her change and her bakery box with a mischievous glint. "I noticed you getting along quite well with a certain handsome man."

She cringed. Yep, she knew this was coming. The shocker was that Colbie hadn't called earlier wanting to know the dish. She pushed the cash drawer shut and went back to folding boxes. "You have romance on the brain, Cole."

"I do. It's a fatal flaw." If she looked momentarily sad, it was only for an instant and in a flash it was gone. But the truth of it remained unsaid between them. Colbie wanted romance for others because of the simple fact she could not have it for herself. No man in his twenties was looking to get saddled down with a disabled mother-in-law and more medical debt than most folks could shoulder.

"Still, I see God's hand in this." Undeterred, Colbie tucked the box under her arm. "Your car could have gotten stolen any time, right? So maybe it is God turning misfortune into victory. Perhaps you were supposed to say yes to the guy when he offered to drive you home. Hel-*lo*."

If only. Just because she knew he was faithful, compassionate, honorable and a dedicated cop didn't mean she had to start hoping. No, she would stay neutral and refuse to see Colbie's take on things. At least this way she didn't have to be afraid of getting hurt, of opening herself up. Of finally meeting someone perfect and finding out she wasn't meant to be loved. That was what she was really afraid of.

Old patterns, her counselor would say.

"Perhaps Billy was the man God meant for me, but he decided not to show up." Equally undeterred, Brianna finished the box and slid it beneath the counter with the others. Deciding she'd done enough to last awhile, she grabbed a clean rag from beneath the counter and the waiting pail of sudsy water. "Unfortunately, that's how free will goes. Now I'm tragically never going to meet my one true love."

"Sorry, I'm not buying it. Which reminds me, I got a text message from Billy."

"Groan." She set the bucket down on the floor and knelt to rinse the cloth in the bleach water. How was she going to convince her sister that the path to true love probably could not start with a blind date? At least, judging by her precious experience. "Billy chickened out."

"No, he said something came up and he had to go out of town on family business. I have a call into him to find out what's going on. I've got to get going." Colbie backed toward the door. "But if you don't think things will work with Mr. Gorgeous Detective, then I can try to reconnect you with Billy."

"As if that wouldn't be a disaster to my self-esteem." Bree rolled her eyes, joking so that Colbie was grinning as she pushed through the door. Her sister's life was somber and filled with hard work, and duty.

Her apron pocket began to vibrate. She dried her hands on her shirt and pulled out her cell. A new text. As Brandi strolled in from the kitchen, balancing a large cake with both hands, Bree scrolled down and opened her new message.

Bree,
I've got a lead on a car. Runs good. Interested?
Max.

Max? She warmed from the inside out, as if she were standing in front of a roaring fire on a cold winter's day. She felt toasty and cozy and glowing. This, from simply thinking about the man.

Max,
I'm interested.
Bree.

"You're shining." Brandi swished around the counter, her apron ruffling with her gait. "Something tells me it's because of a certain detective."

"No comment." If her voice wobbled and she nearly dropped her phone, then it wasn't a sign of significance. She wasn't in love with him or anything. At least, not yet. *Almost,* sure, but not yet. "He's going to help me find a car."

"Whew. Talk about a relief. You need transportation, but the stuff we've waded through online. Scary." That's what Brandi said, but Bree knew she meant something else entirely. "Max is going to be a big help to you. I just know it."

"Me, too." It wasn't the big help thing she was agreeing to. She loved that Brandi always understood her. No words were necessary. There were things too fragile to say out loud and too personal to talk about. Her tender feelings for Max happened to be one of those things. Hopes she didn't dare let flourish, although they were there.

Her phone buzzed again. When she whipped it out of her pocket, there was another text from Max.

Where R U?

She tapped out an answer, aware of her twin watching her with understanding on her face. Brandi knew why Bree's fingers were wooden and her ribs hurt with every breath. This way she felt about Max—what she was trying not to put in words—was entirely new to her. Definitely uncertain ground. That's why it was so terrifying.

At the bakery.

She sent her answer, pocketed her phone and wrung the dishcloth out in the soapy water. Max. She hadn't been able to think of much else. Last night, after the singles event, visions of him interfered with her attempt at late-night studying. He was apparently no match for teaching methods in the elementary classroom. All the workday through, she'd wondered about him. Remembered the rough timbre of his voice. Felt the hurt he hid over his girlfriend's betrayal.

"You're afraid, aren't you?" Brandi hung

close, her whisper loud in the hush of the empty room. "You're afraid to care."

"It's a different kind of afraid." She swiped at the tabletop, scrubbing until it squeaked. "When I was lying in the hospital with tubes and monitors, I was so grateful to be alive. I wanted to play it safe. I never wanted to be hurt like that again."

"Totally expected. You were really hurt, Bree. We didn't know if you would pull through."

"I know." She held fast against the memories trying to well up from the vault she kept them buried in. Collapsing to the kitchen floor, the tile slick and cold beneath her cheek. Charles, the dishwasher, kneeling at her side after the gunmen had left. The anxious tone of the paramedics as they checked her vitals. The tearing sound of the blood pressure cuff, the drone of the helicopter and more pain than she could endure.

"I woke up and realized two things. How gracious God was in sparing me, and how important reaching my dreams were. I've been marking time, too afraid to go after what I want. Afraid that it won't be something I can have."

"A happy life. A loving marriage." Pure understanding, that was Brandi.

"Exactly. There's nothing safe about the kind of relationships we've seen. And I thought—"

"—that a better quality relationship with a solid, decent man would be safe," Brandi finished.

"It looks that way from where we've always stood." She didn't need to tell her twin. Brandi was already nodding as if she knew perfectly.

Bree didn't have to talk about the sting of uncertainty and other people's comments on them and their family before Dad left. And then the unpredictable and often volatile men their mom dated, or married, or divorced. How they would wonder about the kids in school, the ones with the pretty, put-together moms and nice, well-kept cars and their pleasant smiles of greeting and "I love you, have a good day" that seemed as routine as milk and cereal for breakfast. Those kids must have safe, secure lives. It had always looked ideal, as if there were no peril, no risks and no fear.

"Max is a solid guy. Even I can see it." Brandi's reassurance came quietly. "He might be a chance in a lifetime."

"That's exactly why it's so frightening. And hopeful." Did she dare give life to those stubborn wishes, the ones that not even her uncertain childhood or post-traumatic stress could silence?

Max. She felt his arrival like a jolt of electricity, as if jumpstarting a part of her spirit. She turned toward him. Tenderness filled her, sweet as stardust and twice as luminous. She glowed from the inside out, drinking in his dear, dependable presence.

"I'll be in the back. I have cookies to decorate." Brandi slipped away, whispering one last thought. "Don't be afraid of the good kind of love, Bree."

Great advice, but how did she not be afraid? With every step Max took toward her, the panic returned proportionally. The sensation of falling. The vertigo. The struggle to let him close.

The door swung open, and he filled the doorway, shrinking the room, forcing the entire world to vanish. There was only him, just him, and her soul seemed to celebrate. The sunshine gleamed more brightly. The air smelled sweeter. She felt enlivened and happy, and she was no longer falling. She took a step toward him, though she couldn't feel the ground.

"You're a sight for sore eyes." He let the door swing shut behind him, looking ruggedly handsome in black. Black coat, black T-shirt, black jeans. "I had a tough morning."

"You've been working?"

"On the job since six. Got a five-thirty call. Didn't get my beauty sleep." He winked. Strolling closer, she could read the toll the day had taken on his soul. Shadowed eyes, set jaw, a deep weariness that had nothing to do with being woken up early on a Saturday morning. The bruises under his eyes and his unshaken jaw only added proof. "Is that coffee fresh?"

"Just finished brewing." She abandoned her table cleaning and circled around the counter. This time, retreating made no difference in the awareness she felt for him. The bond between them continued, a powerful emotional link that seemed to burrow deep, where she was most vulnerable. She grabbed a to-go cup and filled it with steaming coffee. "Are you sure you want to go car shopping with me? Maybe you want to go home instead."

"No, I'd rather make myself useful." One dimple showed in his lopsided grin, but she could sense something more. He was afraid of this, too, to take a step forward into the dark unknown. There was more meaning to his words, real feeling beneath his attempt at humor. He took the cup she set on the counter and reached for his wallet.

"It's on me. Usefulness has its rewards." She kept her tone light, when she meant more, so much more. "Do you want anything else? A muffin? A cookie. A scone?"

"What's with the muffins?" He frowned at

the display case where the day's baked goods were faced out, to give the customers a good view of their smiling monster faces.

"Do you like my handiwork?"

"You did this to perfectly innocent muffins?"

"And I got paid to do it. Today I decided to go with green-and-pink hair. It seemed to match the springlike day. I like the old-man face the best. It has character." She grabbed a plastic glove with a box on the counter. "Want one?"

"No. Thanks. Too frilly for me, although I like the scowling old guy. You have talent with icing." He tossed a couple bucks in the tip jar and sipped his coffee, keeping watch of her over the rim. "Although the goofy-eyed snaggletooth monster is a close second."

"My job doesn't make the city a safer place the way yours does, but it helps people to smile." She dropped the glove and pushed open the swinging kitchen door. She waved at someone inside the kitchen. "I'm leaving a few minutes early," she said, and let the door brush closed.

"I don't mind waiting if you need to finish your shift, Bree."

"It's been quiet today." She untied her apron and hung it in a small closet. She gathered her coat and purse, and he couldn't keep from cataloguing the graceful way she moved, the precious way she folded a lock of golden hair behind her ear and the luster of her quiet beauty.

"Let me help you with that." He set down his coffee to take her coat and hold it for her.

As she slipped into it, she had to come irresistibly close. Tenderly, he let the experience wash through him. The wonder of her so near that he could see the richer highlight of platinum in her hair, inhale the sugar and icing scent of her, see the sweet vulnerability of her heart. He felt ten feet tall, to her petiteness, and an unprecedented twang of hope vibrated within him as he settled the coat on her shoulders. He wished he could pull her into the shelter of his chest instead of watch as she moved away.

He was not a man ever carried away by his feelings, so what was happening to him?

"What's Marcus up to today?" Her question was light and simple, on the surface.

Just the way he wanted to keep things. Except for the stubborn feelings he couldn't seem to control. Thick, lustrous rays of sunlight followed her as he held the door. Overhead, the bells chimed more sweetly, as if just for her. The mild spring day felt joyful and the images of his morning's work faded from his brain. When he wanted to reach out and take her hand, he settled for walking alongside her instead.

"Marcus is at a friend's house." He opened the passenger door for her, offering a hand to help her up. "Something about a basketball challenge and a video game medley. At least he's out of my hair."

What he meant was, he was glad the kid had friends, the good kind that were a help to him. That he was fitting in well here when the move had originally been traumatic.

"It has to feel good to see him thriving." As if she understood him, she settled on the seat as if she belonged there. "Not many men your age would take on a teenager."

"Teenagers don't scare me. I'm tougher than I look." What he wished he could say was, he's my brother. I would trade my life for his.

Her gaze softened, as if he knew that, too, as if somehow she could see behind the tough exterior and hard-earned armor. He'd never felt so exposed, never felt as understood.

"I'm not at all surprised," she said with an adorable grin. "You look as if you could take on any wrong and win."

"Nah, that's a superhero. I tell you what, I might not win but I give it my best shot." If he kept gazing at her, he was going to lose all possession of his senses. He was going to start believing in goodness again and that she was someone he could trust when the chips were down.

He couldn't seem to stop his fingers from reaching out and brushing at a strand of hair, which had tumbled across her eyes. He couldn't stop the tenderness wrapping him up in knots. Her hair rustled like silk against his callused fingertips, her skin like fine satin.

This is not going to work out, Decker, he told himself. But did that stop him? No. Not one bit. She gazed up at him wordlessly, and he felt lost in her gaze. Lost in those innocent violet depths and her beautiful goodness.

Being with her made his shadows less. His hope more. Overwhelmed by tenderness, he leaned closer. Time slowed, her eyes widened, his pulse flatlined. And in the space between one breath and the next, he leaned nearer, treasuring the tickle of her hair against his jaw and her delicate intake of breath.

Would she move away? Or say no? Or boot him out of her way? To his surprise she didn't. She laid her hand on the center of his chest, a cherished warmth above the place where he had once been so cold. There were no more excuses. No more jokes to crack. Distance vanished between them, and he felt vulnerable.

Armor down, he pressed a kiss to her satiny cheek. He felt her smile and her happiness.

The earth shifted beneath his feet. Barricades built along ago began to crumble inside him, places he had never intended to let anyone in again. But he couldn't help it. As he straightened, and the cool March wind eased between them, he realized he was smiling, too. He didn't know how to tell her what she meant to him, or that he was in, all in. He wanted this to work. The way her hand lingered on his chest for a moment longer before falling away told him she might be feeling the same. Afraid to trust, but unable to hold back her heart.

He shut her door and circled around the truck, taking comfort that at least they were in this together.

Chapter Ten

Happiness hugged her from the inside out. Bree couldn't stop it. She pulled her new ten-year-old economy sedan into the vacant spot in the carport and clapped her hands. She had her freedom back. And her ability to go to and from school, work and church without relying on her sisters or her bike.

A knock rattled her window. She pulled out her keys, grabbed her purse and unlocked the door. Max towered over her, balancing the bags of food and the drink container and still managing to open her door. "How does it feel to have wheels again?"

"Too good to be true."

"Believe it. It's true. Paul's a friend from church. His grandmother can't drive anymore, and I know she took good care of it. You got a great deal."

"Thanks to you, which is why dinner should be on me."

"Not a chance, pretty lady."

Her face heated. She was blushing again. He had that effect on her. He made her feel like a new-and-improved Brianna McKaslin. He made her forget everything she usually worried about. Suddenly she was walking at his side heading for the front door without remembering climbing out of the car or standing on her own two feet or even shutting the car door. Did she lock it? Who knew? That she had forgotten to double check was a sign. Max's kiss had caused her to lose every shred of common sense.

She unlocked the front door and trailed inside, flipping on lights. "You have to remember we are on an extremely small decorating budget. And we're not too tidy. We are when we aren't in school. But when classes are in session, there's not enough time for everything."

"You don't need to apologize." He followed her into the entry hall and pushed the door shut with his elbow. "Typical student apartment, if you ask me."

"Yes. You aren't allowed in the kitchen, though. Brandi left the dishes all over the place. It was her turn to clean up last night. So why don't we go straight to the living room?"

"Sure thing."

She couldn't get their kiss out of her mind. The side of her face tingled, sweetly with the memory. She had never known that a man as tough as Max could be so tender.

Now how was she going to keep counting up all the ways he wasn't right for her? How was she going to stop from falling head over heels, one hundred percent in love with him?

"What's it like having a twin?" He set the food bags and drinks on the scarred coffee table and moved a stack of books aside to make room for the drinks. He nodded toward the framed picture collage on the wall of her and Brandi together.

"I always have someone who understands me perfectly. She's my best friend." Bree settled onto the couch. As long as they spoke of simple things, she would be okay. "She's my constant support. Our lives aren't as similar as they used to be. I went into the elementary teaching program and she went into the secondary, so we don't cross paths like we always used to."

"You used to do everything together?"

"A habit from the crib. We were always together when we were little. We still like the same things, do the same things, watch the same TV shows. It's second nature."

"Must be nice to have someone so close."

"I can't complain." Why was her pulse skipping beats? He moved to the couch and sat on the cushion beside her, his big presence dwarfing her. Her palms went damp. Her brain turned to mush. Little wishes fluttered within her, new and joyful. Wishes that had everything to do with the man at her side.

"I think this is yours." He freed a cup and set it on the table in front of her. It sounded as if he meant something else entirely.

"Yes, it is." She did, too. Afraid to say more and yet wanting more, she took the straw he offered her with whispered thanks.

"Let me say grace." His hand found hers and held on tightly, his rough-warm fingers entwined with hers. It felt romantic sitting at his side, holding his hand and feeling the peace of prayer and the grace of the moment descend.

Show me the way, Father. She bowed her head, watching Max through her lashes as he did the same. *Show me what I do not know.*

A soft joyfulness came to her soul like the kindest song. Reassured, she closed her eyes and let her fears come down.

"Dear Lord…" He began the blessing. She liked the way reverence enriched his voice. He was a deeply faithful man. "Please bless this food and our fellowship. We're asking for Your guidance in our lives and that You lead us to Your purpose, Lord, and strengthen us. Amen."

"Amen." Bree opened her eyes, and all she saw was Max. There was no easy humor to hide behind, no wry joke or distance of any kind. She saw him without shields. Just Max, steel and vulnerability.

"You have a trial coming up fairly soon." He unrolled one of the bags and handed her a cheeseburger.

"In eight weeks. I'm trying not to think of it."

"Are you getting more frequent nightmares?"

"I don't want to say yes, but, well, yes."

"You want to be stronger than that."

He understood. She let out a breath she didn't know she'd been holding, and a surprising amount of tension went with it. She took a fry from the tub he set out. "When you told me that you'd been shot, I should have realized. You went through post-traumatic stress, too."

"Roger that. I still struggle with it from time to time."

"And you feel that's weakness."

"It's certainly not something I like." He reached inside the last bag for his hamburger, paper crinkling, his stoic veneer falling away. "That time I told you about with Nancy's boyfriend, it was the first time I was in real danger.

No doubt about it, I thought I was going to die."

"Sure, because you were shot."

"True." He unwrapped the burger, staring at the silver paper, lost in thought. "He wasn't alone. He had two buddies with him. They waited until I was in my carport. With a cement wall on one side, the house on another, I was essentially trapped. I couldn't get around the car, they were coming from behind me up the driveway. It was pitch-black out, rain falling like hail. That's why I didn't see 'em coming. They were waiting for me, no doubt about that. I remember hearing Manny calling out my name, and that's all the time I had to react. I was hit before I could pull my service revolver. I fell. Never knew concrete could be so hard. Rain was falling sideways, pounding me and I saw the three of them strolling closer to finish the job."

"That had to be terrifying." She went pale, as if she were imagining the scene, or maybe remembering what it felt like to think she was facing the last minutes of her life.

He knew the cost of what violence did to people. He saw it all the time in his line of work. He'd experienced it personally more than once.

"I was fighting as hard as I could to stay

focused. I couldn't move. All I could think was that I had to get my gun, it was my only chance, but I blacked out. " Grim, he remembered the rain staining his face, the grit of the concrete against his cheek, the fiery pain and his heavy, unresponsive body.

"You were lying there unable to defend yourself." Compassion had never looked more authentic. "What happened? They obviously weren't able to—"

She couldn't say the word, bless her.

"No," he said gently. "They weren't able to finish what they started. God must have been watching out for me because my neighbor came home, drove into the shared driveway and I'm told, because of the storm, hit one of the perps. Not bad, just enough to send him flying a few feet. He got up and ran off with the others, and Melvin, a World War II vet, managed to keep me alive until the paramedics showed up."

"God bless Melvin."

"Exactly. I adopted Mel after that. We spent a lot of time together, watching old war movies and playing chess and Scrabble. When he passed a few years later, it was like losing a grandfather." Remembering Mel was an old wound, too, but at least he didn't have to think about those moments lying helpless on the ground, unable to do more than blink and breathe. "It took me nearly a year until I was back to full speed."

"You're very good at that, you know." She set her chin, as if she thought she had him all figured out.

"Good at what?" He took a bite so he wouldn't have to say more.

"I don't know if it's avoidance or denial." She shook her head, scattering tendrils of gold bangs, which fluttered softly against her face.

He resisted the urge to brush her hair from her eyes. Something down deep, call it instinct, wanted him to be nearer to her. To bridge the distance he kept between him and everyone. It would be easy right now to give in and accept her sympathy and her friendship. But he held in his emotions out of habit and the need for safety.

"Probably both," he answered. "It was the first time I was in trouble. Not the last."

"Let me guess. You avoid dealing with it or thinking about it. You put it on the back burner and do what has to be done in your life."

"True. It's working so far."

"You must have nightmares, too."

"It's not so bad these days. I'm not a beat cop anymore. Detective work is harder in some ways. I see tragedy every day, but I've only been shot at once since I got promoted."

"I see that wry grin. Just once doesn't make it any easier."

"What are you trying to get at, pretty lady?" The compliment made her blush.

"Only that it's normal to cope with the trauma after the fact. When I was in the middle of that chaos with guns firing and those meth guys shouting crazy awful things, there was no time to put in perspective what was happening. I was in the moment, that was all, trapped like everyone else in the kitchen." She bit her bottom lip, vulnerable but strong, too. "You've been there more than a few times."

"Except I had training, experience, a revolver and back up. Never underestimate the importance of good buddies who come when you call."

"You're going to have to cope some time."

"Who says I'm not coping? I see the world as it really is and people as they really are." He'd never been more honest with anyone. The experiences had made him hard, tough as nails. He'd learned to be realistic, to accept the fact that there was dark and injustice in this world. It was how he fought against it, solving crimes, methodically piecing bits of information together. His world had become black and white and all the shades of gray in between.

"Max, all it took was one moment. It happened so fast. I nearly lost my life—everything—that night. I wanted to live so badly."

"That's why you fought hard to recover." He knew what that was like, too.

"Yes, I fought as hard as I could. There were surgeries and rehabilitation." She left so much unsaid, but her voice thinned, tremulous with remembering. The memories changed her, making her luminous and achingly real. "When I woke up in the hospital, I had never been so grateful for anything. I still am."

Her words touched him, hooking deep. Sitting beside her in this room surrounded by frilly eyelet pillows and family pictures on the wall, with children's books stuffed into the bookcase and lying out on the coffee table, it was a world apart. A tenacious innocence in spite of what had happened to her. He set down what was left of his burger, shifted on the couch and drank her in. She was like golden sunlight shining into his life, shades of color come to his heart. Everything his battered soul yearned for. Everything he was afraid to believe in.

"When I finally came home from the hospital, I was afraid to go outside." She blushed a little, as if admitting that embarrassed her. "Anything could happen to derail my life and hurt me. Car accidents. Carjackers. A blood clot. Another robbery."

"How did you deal with it?"

"I went out anyway. Because I realized that there is more good in this world—in people—than bad. That is something I will not stop believing."

Respect crashed through him with tidal-wave force. She looked willowy and fragile and far too altruistic to have this happen to her. Worse, she had run straight into danger to resuscitate a shooting victim. Juanita Morales had still died, but he knew things the newspaper didn't. That Brianna had not stopped giving life support until she had fainted from blood loss from her own bullet wound.

He braced hard against it, but emotion came anyway. A new wave of affection powerful enough to knock down his every resistance. The unbreachable walls that had always separated the real part of him from everyone else crumbled like clay. He fisted his hands. He was drowning in a kind of tenderness too enormous to name.

Then the cynical part of him won out. He blinked, trying to bring his thoughts back into focus, back to black and white. She *had* to be too good to be true. After all she'd been through, where was the anger? The disillusionment any crime victim had the right to? And what about her car? Wasn't she upset some joker had stolen from her? What about outrage and the need for justice? "When I look at you and what you've been through, I can't help noticing. You're not angry. You're not bitter."

"Sure. I'm furious that someone decided three restaurant workers' lives were more important than the few thousand of dollars they hoped to get from the safe. I'm angry about the loss of life and destruction two men caused. I lost months of my life." Her chin went up, but there were no tears, just strength. Indomitable steel. "I'm angry that I feel wobbly, that I'm afraid of the dark and that I have to relive it all over again for the trial. But it's not always going to be this way. Those gunmen don't have to change how I see the world or how I see myself. That's what I'm fighting for."

Tears glistened in her eyes but did not fall, the only sign of what this conversation cost her. That beneath the layers of her smiles, her gentleness and her steel remained a pain that may never fully leave.

"I see how hard you are fighting." Captivated, that's what he was. Amazed. Enthralled. In love. He cupped her face in his hands, ready to wipe away those tears should they fall. Wanting to take away her every pain, comfort her and make sure she would never hurt like that again. Commitment to her pounded through him with immeasurable power.

"I won't let them win, not in the end." She leaned her cheek against his hand. "I'm going on with my life. No matter how hard it is, I won't let what happened stop me."

He loved her. There was no fighting it. No altering it. She was hope on a dark night, spring after a bitter winter. Brimming with love for her, both made weak with it and strong by it, he pressed closer, needing to comfort her. Leaving the barriers protecting his heart down, he said the first thing that came to mind. "So, what did you think of my kiss?"

"Your kiss?" Pink crept across her face. A little embarrassed, maybe, but he didn't miss the way she brightened, the same way he did. With hope. "I didn't mind it too terribly much."

"And if I were to kiss you again?"

"I suppose I wouldn't mind that too terribly, either."

"Neither would I." He chuckled once, humor crinkling the corners of his eyes and stealing her heart. As if he heard what she was too shy to say. He leaned closer, still softly cupping her face.

His kiss came gently. A faintest whisper of his lips to hers. Sweetly, she let her eyes drift shut, savoring her first real kiss. She felt the faintest tremble in his hands cradling her jaw, the slight roughness of his whiskers to her skin and a velvet caress as he kissed her again.

Absolute perfection.

After their amazing first kiss, Bree and Max finished their dinner, turned on the television to a classic TV station and watched reruns of a popular fifties' set sitcom. She couldn't remember a more perfect evening—there was that word again—as she laughed out loud with Max's arm around her shoulder.

The front door opened around eight o'clock. Bree exchanged looks with Max as the sounds of keys dropping on the floor, an exasperated "oops" and a thud of a backpack hitting the linoleum rose above the canned laughter from the screen.

"Brandi," she told him unnecessarily, interested to see if he was going to move away from her on the couch.

He didn't.

"Bree?" came Brandi's voice from the other side of the wall. "What a night. Be glad you were off. The Young Life group dropped by, along with about three birthday parties. Total catastrophe." Brandi skidded around the corner, she took in the man sitting on the couch and her jaw dropped in momentary shock. "Oh, I didn't know you had company. Hi, Max. Sorry to interrupt. Just color me embarrassed and I'll tiptoe back the same way I came—"

"Not necessary." He moved away, leaving her side.

It felt lonely without him so near.

"I should get going. It's getting late, and I'm picking Marcus up in the morning and taking him to the early-risers service." He rose to his six-foot-plus height, hovering over her. There was a silent message etched on his handsome face, one she understood. He didn't want the evening to end.

Neither did she. She would be happy to freeze time and spend eternity snuggled at his side, laughing along with Max at the show's story line.

"No, don't go. I spoiled it for you two." Brandi looked tortured. "Pretend I'm not here. I'm going straight to my room. Don't mind me."

Bree watched her twin disappear in a blink. The departing pad of sneakers through the kitchen was so fast, it was too late to call her back.

"I take it your sister isn't used to coming home and finding men in the living room?"

"You know she isn't." Why was she blushing? Did he think she had kissed any other guy in this living room? "All those blind date setups, remember? Isn't that a clue?"

He chuckled, as if he thought that was funny. He held out his hand. "Come walk me to the door."

"Did I thank you for dinner?"

"You did."

"Did I thank you for helping me find a reliable car?" She placed her hand in his, palm to palm, locking her fingers with his. A perfect fit. It felt right as they each went separate ways around the little coffee table and met again in the middle of the living room, hands still together.

"I'm sure you could have done a fine job on your own, but I wanted to help." His tone deepened, dropping low and intimate, as if there was more he couldn't say.

There was more she couldn't say, too. Like how much it meant that he had been there for her. That he had checked under the car's hood himself, helped to negotiate the price, and most important of all, she felt one hundred percent safe with him.

The apartment was small, so a few more steps took them into the entry hall, where Brandi's backpack remained slumped against the wall. Bree found her gait slowing to minuscule steps. Max did, too.

"How would you rate the evening, on a scale of one to ten?"

His question made her blush. "I'm not sure how to answer that."

"The kisses aside." Mischief twinkled in his stunning blue eyes. "Did you like being with me?"

Talk about putting her heart on the line! She froze, wondering how she could open up like that. She was mostly experienced with shielding her feelings, not in exposing them.

"The truth, Bree." Soft, his words. More caring than she could have imagined. "If it helps, I would rate being with you a fifty on a scale of ten."

"Me, too." So she wasn't alone. Her slow smile stretched her face, but it didn't come close to the enormity of the happy glow welling through her.

"Good. Then how about going to dinner with me next Friday?" He shrugged into his leather jacket, looking calm and unruffled and intensely manly.

Dinner, as in a date. This evening had been totally casual, but a date was something else. Something more. If it were a dream, she would have blithely and coolly accepted, made some witty banter and captured his entire heart with her smile.

Reality: her brain turned to fog. Her tongue forgot every word of the English language. She realized she was still grinning ear to ear.

"Maybe." It was the best she could do. She was not coy. She was mostly too shy to say anything more.

"Then maybe I'll be here at six." He searched her face, serious and intense, and she felt the tug of the connection between her heart and his. A click of understanding crinkled in the corners of his eyes. He understood what she could not say. How much this meant to her. How risky it was to fully open her heart for the first time.

"Me, too," he assured her, as his lips grazed her cheek.

A burst of sweet affection blazed through her like a star falling from the night sky. Too overwhelmed with emotion, buoyant with hope, she could only waggle her fingers at him in goodbye as he opened the door. How was it that he could understand her without words? She thought she could feel the same vulnerable hope within him as he smiled one last time and closed the door.

"Is he gone?" Brandi whispered a few seconds later.

Bree nodded, realizing her sister was peering around the kitchen archway. "You didn't have to scamper off. You could have stayed and talked with Max, too."

"Yeah, but I really want things to work out for you. He had his arm around you." Brandi emerged and flipped on the kitchen light, unfortunately highlighting the backlog of dirty dishes. She was very skilled at ignoring them as she grabbed a soda from the fridge. "Do you want one?"

"Please." Bree sidled up to the breakfast bar and moved a stack of books out of the way so she could sit on one of the chairs. "He's nice, isn't he?"

"Super nice. I'm so excited about you two. I can hardly stand it." Now it was Brandi's turn to grin ear to ear as she popped the top on both cans and set them on the counter. She hopped into the other seat. "I tried not to overhear, I really did, but there's poor insulation in this place. He asked you out."

"He did." She still couldn't believe tonight. The kisses. The closeness. The sweetness. "I'm dating Mr. Dreamy."

"See? I told you. I've been praying hard for you, Bree. I told you there wasn't a reason why you couldn't find a great guy. He's your happily-ever-after."

"You say that with such confidence. We're going to have to wait and see. Happily-ever-after takes time, not to mention all the pitfalls on the road along the way." She sipped the cool grape soda, savoring it. "I'm starting to hope, Brandi. I mean, to really hope."

"I know. He seems like such a great guy. Raising his brother like that. The way he treats you. And, oh, the way he looks at you."

"Like how?"

"Like you are his dream come true." Brandi slurped her soda, sparkling with excitement. "Do you want to know what my devotional verse was today?"

"I'm afraid to ask." Afraid? She was back up on that mountain, except the glacier at her feet had stopped cracking. It was holding, and she was able to take a look around and glimpse the tiniest view of forever. The possibility of this working out with Max. Of their love deepening. Of an engagement ring, marriage and spending her evenings at his side, snuggled close and laughing at the same things together, at the exact same moment.

"Here. Listen to this." Brandi had dug a book out from one of the dozen on the counter and read from it. "Jeremiah 31:13. *I will turn their mourning into gladness; I will give them comfort and joy instead of sorrow.* This is the Lord leading you, Bree. Don't be afraid to follow where He takes you."

Her throat filled with a tangle of emotions, all new and terrifying, the strongest of which was hope. She sipped her soda, trying to wash away the feelings. But they remained, like Scripture said, a comfort and joy.

Chapter Eleven

"What is up with you?" Marcus burst into the kitchen with his ear buds hanging around his neck and audible hip-hop music vibrating through them. He tossed the key ring on the counter. "Are you going to church tonight or something?"

"Or something." Max grabbed the iPod out of Marcus's sweatshirt pocket and turned the dial.

"Hey! Don't mess with the tunes." The kid protested with a grin.

"I'm messing with the volume." He shoved the contraption back at the boy. "Don't make me sorry I'm leaving tonight. What have you got planned?"

"I cleaned up the garage and the truck like you wanted, so I get to watch TV tonight, right?"

"I picked up some rental movies for you. They're in by the television."

"Did you get that action movie I wanted to see?"

"I did." Fortunately, it had a PG-13 rating.

"Sweet."

Max grabbed the key ring from the counter. If he was nervous about tonight, he didn't want to admit it. He especially didn't want the kid to know. "I've already paid for the pizza. It should be here in ten. Tip money for the driver is by the door."

"Aye, aye, Captain." Marcus stuck in his ear buds. "You never said. You got a church function?"

"No." Max grabbed his coat off the back of one of the kitchen chairs. "None of your business, kid."

"Ah, with a little deductive reasoning, I can figure this out." He leaned backward against the countertop and crossed his arms over his chest, looking satisfied with himself. "You've got a date tonight with the lovely Brianna, don't you?"

"No comment." The kid was going to make a big deal out of this, and Max was psyched out enough as it was. He hadn't been on a serious date in years. Blind dates aside, it had been well before Marcus had come to live with him. Three, maybe four years ago.

"Ah-ha! Your face tells the story." He hooted with victory. "You like her, don't you?"

"Again, no comment." One glance at the kitchen clock told him he had best get moving. "You know the rules. No one over. You don't leave the house. You don't answer the door except for the pizza guy. You go to bed at ten o'clock if I'm not home."

"I know, I know." The kid rolled his eyes. "Don't you worry about me, bro. Just concentrate on charming the lovely Brianna. You've got a shot at actually getting a girlfriend this time. No more lone wolf. I'm proud of you, buddy."

Max rolled his eyes as Marcus clapped him on the shoulder, a perfect imitation of every time he had been proud of the boy. "Go watch your movie."

That's what he said, but what he meant was, thanks. They both knew it as he stepped foot into the garage.

Wow, it really was clean. The kid had done a decent job. Impressed, Max whipped open the truck door, his thoughts already turning to his date tonight.

Brianna. No doubt he'd fallen for her. Just because he was a tiny bit in love with her didn't mean he had to go charging down that road at full speed. No, he would take his time before he decided if he would let himself be drawn to her any further. He had iron self-control and steely self-discipline. He wasn't one of those men who got carried away by too much feeling, and that would serve him well now.

He jammed the key into the ignition and listened to the struggle of the engine to start. Not the best sign, but then it turned over and he was good to go. He backed out of the garage, a little nervous.

Lord, please let this go well tonight. No more date disasters. If there is one, I'm going to take it as a sign. I'm not looking to get hurt again. He checked for traffic before pulling out onto the main road, realizing too late he was heading in the wrong direction.

If he was looking for a sign, there it was. He was more in love with Bree than he wanted to admit. He was a levelheaded guy, and look at him, taking the wrong road, dating a woman who was entirely wrong for him, a storybook sweetheart. He didn't believe in fairy tales.

That didn't stop his nerves popping through him like cola bubbles. Tonight meant more than he wanted to admit. Much more. He turned into a bank parking lot and oriented the truck in the right direction.

Bree stood in her kitchen, going through her nicest purse. "Cell phone, driver's license, hair brush, front door key. Looks like I'm ready to go."

Her words echoed in the still kitchen and

sounded really nervous. Maybe because that's exactly what she was. So nervous, she couldn't get the zipper closed and dropped her bag. It tumbled to the floor and she knelt to grab it, and dropped it. Again.

Nice. Way to play it cool.

The doorbell rang. He's here! That single thought stirred up her panic again. One hundred percent, suffocating, blind panic. Max Decker was out of her realm of experience. Dating him was uncharted territory. She had never cared about a man so much.

Scary stuff. Neat, but scary.

He's waiting, Bree. She dashed through the kitchen and caught her reflection in the wall mirror on the way by. Okay, now she was worried even more. She was plain Brianna McKaslin in really nice clothes and cute shoes. When she opened the door what would Max see? Would he look at her and see her flaws? She could certainly see them clearly. Each and every one.

Suddenly this date didn't sound like a good idea. Why couldn't she be one of those confident kinds of girls who breezily handled any situation? Something always went wrong on her dates, and she *so* didn't want that to happen with this one. She liked Max. She didn't want a date gone wrong to drive him away. She wanted this to work out. More than anything.

Her shoes tapped across the entryway, and a tight ball of worry remained lodged in between her ribs. She took a deep breath, staring at the doorknob when the text from Romans in her morning's devotional hopped into her thoughts. *May the God of hope fill you with all joy and peace as you trust in him, so that you may overflow with hope by the power of the Holy Spirit.*

She clasped the doorknob, the metal felt cool in her hand that no longer shook. She needed to stay full of joy and peace. She would trust this would work out right, no matter what.

The door swung open and she was surprised at how calm she sounded. "Hello, Max."

He looked great with rain glistening in his dark hair and along the impressive line of his shoulders. He held a vase of a dozen perfect red rosebuds. As she opened the door wider, allowing him to step inside, he was even more handsome in a black sweater and trousers. A total dream.

"These are for you." No dimples this time. No flash of his dazzling grin. He simply watched her steadily with a quiet question.

"Thank you. These are lovely." He'd brought flowers. He stood before her with his heart open, waiting for her to do the same. She wanted to choose the safest route and to breezily talk of surface things: the roses, the weather, the busy week she'd had. It would be safer to stick to those subjects and keep him at arm's length.

It wasn't what Max's silent question was asking.

Her hands trembled again as she took the crystal vase. His hands curled over hers, holding her captive for a few sweet moments. His hands were callused and strong; he was a hard-working man. Her instinct was to withdraw and move away, to break the contact he was trying to make. Run, that's what she'd learned to do. Escape, because distance was safer. Max was too close. Not just in proximity but also in a way much more personal.

She stayed; not only in accepting his hands anchoring hers, but in her heart. She did not close up. She did her best to stay in the moment, in feeling what could not be said with words. It was like cracking open a door to her heart, one that had never been unlocked before. Vulnerable and frightened, she gazed up at him and wondered, did he feel this way, too?

His fingers released hers, and she backed away. The closeness remained, and so did the defenselessness. She set the flowers onto the little entry table. "What's Marcus up to tonight?"

"Pizza and a DVD. That should keep him

busy until I get home." He stepped into the foyer and took her coat from the open closet. "You look beautiful tonight."

She wanted to say something humorous, anything to put distance between them and slam closed the barely opened door to her deepest self. But she couldn't. His serious, searching gaze focused on her as he shook out her best wool jacket. Caring deepened the fabulous blue of his irises as he held her jacket for her.

Her stomach twisted hard. With muscles quaking and her feet unsteady, she slipped her arms into the sleeves. Her breathing halted as he inched closer to settle the garment in place over her shoulders. So near, and it wasn't physical. His hands curved over her shoulders, making her feel cozy and cared for.

Wow, her soul said. Absolute wow.

"Th-thank you." Her words sounded way too breathy and dizzy.

He stepped away, but the dizzy sensation remained.

"Are you ready?" He paused in the doorway, framed by the darkening evening and charcoal clouds, his hand held out to her.

Because there was a crack in her heart that hadn't been there before, she knew he was really asking her something else entirely. Not, was she ready to go on the date?—but was she ready to go on this new, uncertain journey with him?

"Yes." She fit her hand to his bigger one. Relief crossed his face, and only then did a grin tease the corners of his mouth. He drew her onto the step with him and closed the door. She double-checked that the lock had caught— okay, a habit that was never going to go away apparently—and let him lead her down the stairs and onto the walkway.

"My brother is tickled you and I are going out tonight." He hit his remote and the truck's doors unlocked. "What does the bookstore sister have to say about all this?"

"She's convinced she had a hand in it."

"Because of the singles night the two of them conspired to get us to?" He opened her door.

"Colbie is sure that helped. You have to excuse her. She has a romantic soul." She hopped onto the high truck seat with the help of his hand at her elbow.

"I imagine she has a rough time of it." He grabbed the buckle and pulled it out for her. "I don't have to be a detective to get that Colbie's mom needs a lot of care, and your sister is the one who has to look after her."

"She has a hard road, it's true." So many shields that were up, guarding the susceptible places within. He knew, because he was no different. She smiled gently. "But Colbie says she doesn't mind. What she does for her mom is out of love."

"Sounds like she's definitely related to you." Why was he smiling? He had learned from experience. He kept his feet on the ground and his expectations reasonable. Which was smart and sensible. Nothing wrong with that.

None of it explained why he loved her. Or why he started to hope he could have everything with her—marriage, kids, growing old sitting on the porch, knowing he could always trust her. Her unguarded violet eyes watched him with silent hope, and it was like a punch to his soul.

Hold on to your heart, man. He closed her door and hiked around the front of the truck. With every step he took, he kept her in his sight. She looked more incredible to him with every passing moment. Demure and modest in a simple black dress and a dark wool coat, she was a rare and precious treasure he was afraid of losing.

Take this one step at a time. Don't look ahead. Don't expect the worst. The last time he'd been this at risk was when he'd been on that rainy driveway with a bullet next to his spine.

The wind gusted, cold and biting, as he opened the door. He hardly noticed it as he hopped in, wanting to be with her. His spirit turned toward her, and the tie he felt to her was something like the force of gravity holding the earth to the sun.

He gave the key a turn. Nothing happened. No click. No engine sounds. Not even a puff from the defroster. "This can't be good. Let me try again."

He did. Again, nothing. The truck was dead. Great. He thought of Marcus cleaning out the truck and vacuuming it. Had the kid run the battery down playing CDs?

"It's a sign." Bree bit her bottom lip, as if she were trying to keep from laughing. "Already. We haven't even gotten to the restaurant yet. A lot of things can go wrong at the restaurant. Messed-up reservations. A table by the kitchen door or by someone loud and obnoxious. It could be closed. There could be a grease fire."

"I knew this was too good to be true. Here I thought we had bypassed the first-date-disaster scenario. We had burgers in your living room last week. That turned into a date. In my book, that counts as date number one."

"Apparently you are wrong." When laughter lit her up, she was a dream come true. Luminous inner sparkle and soul-deep beauty.

Face it, man. You aren't just a little bit in love with the woman. He rubbed his hand over his face, trying to make his gray matter work. Trying to figure out how to salvage the evening.

"I didn't want a dead battery. That's why I tossed Marcus's iPod at him when he was cleaning up the garage. I should have known better. I don't want this to be the start of a downhill slide for the evening."

"I'm afraid it is, Max. You have to be realistic."

"Realistic? This from Miss Optimism?"

"I'm *realistically* optimistic. " Her hair was tied back in a fancy braid, softly sleek against her head, leaving artful curls framing her oval face. The sweetest sight. It took all his effort to pay attention to her words, for he was wrapped up in the loving tenderness filling him up, changing him.

"We may as well embrace the doom," she was saying. "Just accept things might not go according to plan."

"And that makes it better how?" Distantly, he gave the key one more turn one more try to no avail. The battery was totally dead. What was foremost to him was the current of emotion, like a tide coming in, making deep sparking pools out of shadowed places. He left the key in the ignition. "Stay here. I'll just pop the hood and take a look. Maybe a terminal is loose and it will be an easy fix."

"Optimism. That's more like it. Guess what? It's starting to rain."

Sure enough, droplets landed on the windshield, smearing it. Big raindrops. Wind-driven raindrops. Falling fast, and before he could blink, water sluiced down the windshield, obliterating all view of the outside. The rain hit so hard it sounded like quarters being thrown on the truck's roof.

"Max, I have another solution. My car isn't nearly as spiffy as your truck, but the battery works and it runs."

"Good idea." He grabbed his keys and reached for the umbrella he kept under the seat. It was way too late to keep his feet on the ground and his expectations reasonable. He leaned across the console and brushed a thumb across the side of her face, a tender gesture. Devotion left him trembling as he pressed a kiss to her cheek.

Her wide eyes held all the emotions he was trying not to feel. A little terror, a lot of hope and more love than he felt safe with.

Too late to hold back his heart. It was no longer his.

"Max, you didn't by any chance listen to a weather report today, did you?"

"No, why?" One dimple flashed as he slowed for a stoplight.

"Gee, I wonder." She bit her lip to keep from laughing. The stoplight was barely more than a red blur through the fog and rain. The car's defroster couldn't keep up with the dampness, right along with the windshield wipers. Thunder crashed overhead like a marching band. "Is it my imagination, or do I hear running water?"

"No, I hear it, too." He opened the door to take a peek. The faint drone became a coursing current. "That explains it. We're experiencing some minor street flooding."

"Minor? That looks pretty major to me."

"Sure, but I didn't want to startle you. Maybe we should get off this street." He closed the door, shook his head and water droplets flew off the ends of his hair. The red blur of the streetlight remained.

Lightning snaked across the black smear of sky. Thunder cannoned overhead, shaking the windows in their casings. Hilarity rumbled in his voice. "I think the storm's getting worse."

"Do you think? And the light is still red."

Raindrops changed to hail, clattering down from the heavens like a billion ball bearings firing against the car. Rounds of ice hurled everywhere, drowning out all other noises—including the rushing sound of the minor flash flood.

"I've lost sight of the road. Can you tell if the light's changed?"

"No." This wasn't funny was it? Why was

she laughing? "I can't even see the blur now. I think there's something you didn't test when you went over my car with that fine-tooth comb."

"You had to go and point that out, didn't you?" Hail was accumulating on the lower surface of the windshield, the wipers swiping at a slow and dignified speed—their only working setting—were only compacting it into a sheet of impenetrable ice. "You wouldn't happen to have an ice scraper in here, would you?"

"No, as this is the first ice incident I've experienced since owning the car."

He shook his head, chuckling. "This won't take long. I'm going to go knock the ice off so we can see to drive."

"What are you going to use?"

"I'm thinking my shoe." He put the car in park. "You stay here where it's warm and dry. I won't be long—"

"Max? I think I see something out the side window."

"Don't tell me it's a tornado. We've got enough weather-related disasters for one date." He winked.

"Realistically, what are our chances of getting to the restaurant?"

"Across town, with street flooding, marginal windshield wipers and—" Thunder exploded, shaking the car. The speed and weight of the hail increased, drowning out all noise. He stuck his head out the window. Hail the size of gumballs bounced into the car. He had to shout to be heard above the clatter. "If the storm doesn't get worse, maybe ten percent? The good news is that the light just changed."

"I spotted a neon restaurant sign on my side of the street. We should pull over. Wait—" She unrolled her window, despite Max's protests. A whirlwind of icy balls hurled against her, stinging her face and bruising the top of her head. She checked the road behind them. Since she didn't see any headlights coming—none that she could see in the torrential storm anyway—she waved him over.

"I can't see." Chuckling, Max lowered his window again. "This is a dating first. You sure you don't want me to take you home and call it a disaster?"

"It's too early to give up hope. Besides, you couldn't drive me that far. The weather's too bad."

"You're right. Head in. Hang on. I can't see where I'm going."

Since her face felt frozen, she didn't argue. Hail pounded her little car as they crept across the width of a lane. "I still don't see anyone coming. I think we're safe."

"Sure, because no one else wants to drive in

this," he quipped with his head out the window. He navigated toward what he thought was the driveway—it was—and slid through the nearly empty parking lot. A green gleam appeared faintly at first, and grew stronger as he approached; it was the sign above Mr. Paco's Tacos front door. He angled the vehicle so she would be protected by the awning. "You go in where it's warm. I'll park and follow you in."

"I don't mind waiting for you, Max. Look at me. It's not like this can get much worse." She swept orbs of hail out of her wispy curls. Ice mantled the collar and shoulder and right arm of her coat, making her look like a snow woman. Her face had turned gently pink from the cold and her hyacinth-colored irises brightened with life and laughter.

Adoration ripped through him, tearing him down and making him strong at the same time. "Brianna, go inside for me, please."

"Look who's getting bossy."

"Just trying to take care of you, darlin'."

"I see that." Her lightheartedness faded. Her smile vanished, leaving only quiet between them.

The hail continued to beat at the car, and he brushed melting ice out of his eyes. A globule oozed beneath his collar and trailed down the back of his neck, but he hardly cared because she leaned across the seat and pressed a kiss to his jaw. Softly, her hand touched his, the connection deepening between them, eking behind his cracked armor, which never had a chance against her.

"I'll be inside, then." She grabbed her purse, buttoned her coat and opened the door, unaware of what she'd done to him.

Affection so powerful it hurt seized him, heart and soul. He was just one man, helpless to stop it.

I love you way too much, pretty lady. Although the curtain of hail swallowed her, he could feel her by the tug of his heart and by the pull of the bond his love for her made.

Chapter Twelve

Bree dragged a deep-fried Tater Tot through the cup of hot salsa and popped it into her mouth. She might be soaked through and her carefully done hair was a total mess, but the evening wasn't an actual loss. There wasn't much a bucket of Mr. Paco's Mexi-fries couldn't improve.

For instance, take the man across from her. He might be rain soaked, and his dark hair may still be periodically dripping, but he was here with her. What could be better?

"So, what were your real plans for tonight?" Call her curious, but she had to know.

"You mean the plans that were rained out?" He unwrapped his second beef taco.

"Maybe they were never meant to be."

"Can't argue with that." He took a bite, crunching into the crispy corn shell.

He was different from any guy she had ever met before. Aside from the responsible, capable thing he had going on, he was infinitely calm. Any number of guys she could think of—including her own brothers—would have lost his temper at least once during his attempt to drive in the blizzard of hail with his head out the window. Not Max. He had to be more drenched through than she was—he'd come into the restaurant looking like the abominable snowman—but his temperament was the same as always, a little wry, a little amused and stalwart.

He was not Mr. Dreamy. No, that title no longer cut it. He was Mr. Awesome, bordering on incredible. The man was too great for words. He had to have some faults, right? She unwrapped her chicken taco and tore open a packet of salsa.

"I don't know that look on your face," he commented from across the table, repositioning his taco to take another bite. "I'm almost afraid to know what you're thinking."

"It's about you, and you're not going to like it." She upended the packet and squeezed. "What flaws are you hiding? You have to have at least one."

"Are you kidding? I think I'm one big flaw."

"I'm sure I'll agree with you eventually." Being with him, talking and joking and making reasons to laugh was beyond her experience and was straight out of her dreams. This was a wish she had been too afraid to cling to, for fear it could never actually come true. She felt relaxed enough with the closeness they shared to kid him a little more. "Men become more flawed over time, at least that's my experience."

"It's true. I've heard the same comment before." If he was no longer jesting, only a faint flash of shadows hinted at it, and then it was gone. His gaze was warm again, his eyes crinkling pleasantly in the corners. "If you listen to Marcus, I'm a lone wolf. I could chill when it comes to his grades. I 'harsh his mellow' because I won't let him blast music in the house. I'm not cool because I won't let him get his own wheels."

"I can see that about you. There are more flaws than I realized." She tossed the packet aside. That he was raising his half brother happened to be one of the things she loved about him. One of about a dozen things. She was adjusting to being close to him. To being open to the remarkable relationship blooming between them. "So, name a few more. Do you have bad credit? Terrible follow-through? Gamble? Avoid commitment?"

"No. Sometimes. Never. Who knows?" A

bunch of taco innards tumbled onto his blue plastic tray. He didn't seem to notice as he was focused on her. Judging by his smirk, he was having fun, too. "I admit I haven't committed to a woman yet, as in proposed, but that doesn't mean I'm not capable of it. I could step up."

"So, that's a maybe on the commitment phobia?"

"Who isn't afraid of commitment? It's a scary thing. You let down your guard, you make yourself vulnerable. You can get hurt, and hurt bad."

"I can't argue with that. It scares me, too." She might be scared, but she wasn't going to let it chase her away. This, between them, meant too much. Max meant too much.

"It's good to know we're in this together, then." He could make her forget her name when he gazed at her like that, with the full power of his soul. "As for my other flaws? I work too much. I like to seize possession of the TV remote."

"I already knew that." She took a bite out of the end of her taco, feeling the shell crack apart. Pieces of chicken, salad and cheese slipped through her fingers.

"If this is an interrogation, it's your turn to reveal your flaws." He scooped the insides of his taco back into the shell with his fingers. "You don't have any, do you?"

"Uh, hello? I had a panic attack in front of you that first evening we met, remember?"

"It wasn't so bad. You were just a little shaky."

"It felt like more than that." Sure, they were keeping things light, but she stored a lot of fears down deep. That the P.T.S. would get worse instead of better, that she would always be marked by the robbery the same way she feared her childhood had. That this happiness with Max was simply a borrowed moment in time, treasured but not meant to last. That she was somehow not good enough to love and be loved the way she prayed to be. Too may flaws. Not wanting to go *there*, she turned her taco, studying the crack down the middle, trying to figure out a strategic way to eat it. "I would call flashing back an enormous fault. Gigantic. Enormous. Wouldn't you?"

"No." Ironclad compassion, that's what she saw. "I've been there. I've stood in that place when your world is no longer safe. I know that when you're in a situation, whatever the trauma is, you've got two choices. To fold, or to stand. To let it break you, or to overcome it."

Footsteps padded their way, and Max fell silent. She realized someone was coming through the empty dining area. She blinked until her eyes focused and she could make out

Mr. Paco, carrying a tray with several different things on it. He was a friendly, middle-aged man with salt-and-pepper hair and distinguished looks.

"Hi, Max. Hello there, Miss McKaslin. It's a slow night, so I thought I would bring by more Mexi-fries and tacos. Compliments of the house." He slid the tray on the end of the table. "I hope everything is good?"

"It's great, thanks." Bree had always harbored a soft spot for Mr. Paco. He seemed to be everything a good father should be. "I saw Isabella in the library yesterday. I miss having classes with her."

"She studies very hard and does well in school, but she has changed her major again." With an indulgent smile, Mr. Paco nodded and backed away. "Let me know if you need anything else."

They thanked the man together, and it was an odd sensation listening to Max's deep tones blend with hers.

"His daughter used to be in the teaching program with me," she explained after Mr. Paco departed, "but she decided teaching wasn't for her."

"That was nice of him to bring more food." Max gestured toward the window, which was foggy on the inside. Outside was a heavy, driving rain and hail combo that hadn't done much to melt the ice in the parking lot, but added to the street flooding.

Even from where she sat in the middle of the restaurant, she could see the current running down the middle of the road. Good thing they decided to stay here. Funny, how things worked. It wasn't the destination, but the journey. Being with him was what mattered. This man with his strength, humor and understanding was her paradise on earth—even if they were sitting in Mr. Paco's Tacos.

But what were the chances he felt the same way about her? She had climbed high out of her comfort zone. She had to trust he would not let her fall.

"I've figured out another flaw of yours." He dunked a Mexi-fry in the salsa cup. There was both a hint of levity in his tone and the weight of earnestness.

"Do tell." She could feel the layers of humor over the serious. To talk on one level, and sense on another that was pure emotion. To know he had meant what he said about being strong and standing tall. That they were the same that way.

"You're perfect," he confessed.

"Far from it, trust me." She adored him for thinking it, but he was sadly mistaken. "I've got about five hundred flaws, a half a ton of baggage I'm dragging around with me and post-traumatic stress disorder."

"Like I said, perfect."

It was as if their hearts had met in the middle, as if their souls had taken a step closer.

The urge to bolt returned. Tiny tremors crept through her, into her spirit, and she tried to hide it. She took a tiny bite, her taco cracked completely and tumbled onto her tray. Sauce dripped down her chin and she grabbed for a paper napkin. Vaguely she was aware of the front door whooshing open, letting in a gust of wintry wind and the blizzarding drum of hail and rain and another customer. All she could focus on was Max's deep voice murmuring, "Let me." His napkin brushed her chin.

The burst of pure love she felt from him brought tears to her eyes. It was a small gesture on the surface, but it resonated through the layers below. She felt his meaning and the truth of his heart. I love you, he'd said.

"Thank you." What she meant was, I love you, too.

Comprehension crossed his face. He softened, as if more of his defenses had gone down. The smile stretching his dimples had nothing to do with humor. His loving gaze latched on to hers, and the intensity of it was like a shocking pain. It was hard being ever more vulnerable, but she did not blink, she did not fold, she did not move away. She let him see her down to the soul, closer than anyone had been before.

Max closed the passenger door in the dim shadows of her carport and considered the woman at his side. She fussed at her buttons, getting them straight before folding her hand-knit scarf around her neck.

Emotions gathering within him stung, both gentle and intense. Like warmed honey, they oozed into the hurt places he hadn't thought about in a long time. He hadn't loved a woman since Nancy; he hadn't let himself. And if there was a tiny voice at the back of his head whispering to him how this couldn't last, he did his best to silence it.

He wanted this to work. He wanted the chance to love Brianna for the rest of his life. He sure hoped that was God's plan for him. He'd simply have to wait and see.

He held out his hand. "That wasn't too bad, as far as possible date disasters go."

"I agree." She slipped her small hand in his. "It definitely could have been worse."

"At least most of the hail melted and the drains caught up with the rain, or we would have been swimming home." He said that just to make her chuckle, a melodic trill that had to be one of his favorite sounds. "Here's the true test. Any chance this will lead to another date?"

"I would say fair to middling." She moved with unconscious grace. He liked the way each movement rolled into the next, almost like an unpretentious ballet.

"Just fair to middling?" He knew she was pulling his leg. Easy to tell by the quiet joy twinkling in her like the stars peering through the clouds overhead.

"All right. I think it's safe for you to assume I would say yes to another date." She blushed, dipping her chin as if to take care to avoid the stick spots on the walkway, but he wasn't fooled. He felt the emotions she didn't want him to see.

Yeah, me too, he thought. Not trusting his voice, afraid the depth of his love for her—his vulnerability to her—would be fully revealed, he kept silent. Walking beside her without words was just fine. In harmony, her lighter step tapped with his heavier one. Their shadows, one short, one taller trailed ahead of them up the stairs.

The clouds tore apart and it felt as if moonlight spilled down just to light their way. Melting ice trickled from the roof and flowerbeds and became a musical accompaniment as he unlocked the door. Hard to believe the way she stared up at him with unveiled love. Hard to think this had a chance of lasting.

"Do you want to come in for some tea?" Awash with silvered light, she captivated him ever more. The moonlight turned her golden hair to burnished platinum, her creamy complexion to pearl, her goodness to purity.

He loved her so much. Too much. When he was with her, she disarmed him. Completely, utterly unprotected, he took a step back from his fairy tale. "I would love to stay, but it's late. I have Marcus to check on."

"Right." Her regard for him did not appear to dim when faced with the reality of his responsibilities. "What about your truck?"

"I think the tow truck I called has already come and gone. All should be well when I go to start it this time. Thanks for volunteering your car for our mission." He couldn't resist reaching out, against all common sense, and stirring the silken light that was her hair.

Love was changing him. Like dawn touching darkness, he was no longer the same as he'd been five minutes ago. When he brushed his fingertips along the perfect slope of her face, from cheekbone to jaw, reverence blazed through him like a meteor tumbling from the sky.

Believe, his soul whispered. Just believe.

"Thank you for a wonderful time." Her smile could stop the earth from turning.

"Tonight was my pleasure," he said gruffly. "I was glad we kept this from becoming just one more date disaster."

"Me, too." She gently, slightly, leaned her cheek against his hand, the one he could not move away from her. Warmth tingled from his fingertips, as wondrous as the stars above.

Never had he felt like this. Never had he experienced love powerful enough to carry him away. He brushed a kiss to her lips, and that was like starlight, too.

"You're trembling." Concerned, he took her by the hand. "You're cold?"

"Not too cold." Shyly, she blushed.

"It's the dark. I should have realized." He pulled her into his arms, cradling her against his chest, right where she belonged. He kissed the top of her head, emotion burning in his throat. "I know you don't feel safe in the dark."

"You're right." She tipped her face up, revealing her beautiful love for him lustrously on her face. "But I always feel safe with you."

I feel safe with you, a voice out of his past repeated. The memory seized him, shattering the bliss, hurling him back to the rain-soaked cement when he could not move. Nancy's confession rang, a bitter note from their final discussion at their break up. *That's the reason I dated you, Max. I was safe with you. I thought it would be enough, but it isn't. You need too much from me. I can't love you.*

That wasn't happening this time, right? Max unwrapped Bree from his arms, hating how bereft he felt. The wind gusted, icy enough to make them both shiver. That's not a sign, he stubbornly told himself as he caressed a misplaced lock of hair out of her eyes. Affectionately, she smiled up at him. He could not doubt the way she felt for him.

But was it strong enough? A small voice within him asked. Would it last?

He was wholly involved and too deeply in love with her. If this didn't work out, then he was headed for a terrible fall. A crushing, lethal one.

"It's getting colder." He took the first difficult step away from her and opened her door. "We both better get out of this wind."

"You're right." She hesitated, still shivering, as if the last thing she wanted to do was to part with him.

Me, too, he thought tenderly. He would be happy to spend eternity with her right on this doorstep, but it wasn't practical and he didn't know how this would end. He had to shore himself up just in case. "I'm not sure how the rest of my weekend is going to go. I'll do my best to call and we'll discuss our next date. Deal?"

She smiled at his question, not the most eloquent or revealing. When she laid her palm on his chest, over his heart, he knew she understood. "It's a deal."

There was no need for words as she slipped out of the reach of the moonlight. The platinum of her hair became gold again, the silvered tones faded from her face, but she was as dear to him and always would be.

"Good night, Max." She clung to the edge of the door, too beautiful to believe in and too good to be true.

"Good night, Brianna." He jammed his hands in his pockets. It took all his strength of will to turn his back and force his feet down the slick steps. He heard the door whisper shut and the deadbolt click into place. His world had changed again. No water dripped musically from the roof. The moonlight faded as more clouds moved in. The wet walkway turned to ice.

Without looking back, he climbed into his truck and started the engine. He drove away as the first raindrops fell.

Chapter Thirteen

"You keep checking your phone," Lil commented as she wheeled from their trailer's kitchen with a plate on her lap. "You wouldn't be expecting a call from someone special, would you?"

"Yeah, from a certain ruggedly handsome detective?" Colbie added from her place at the table.

"Did you know he's called her twice since their date last night?" Brandi chimed in as she took the plate Lil offered her.

Brianna knew she was blushing, mostly because she could see her nose turn strawberry red. Great. Way to hide your feelings, Bree. She added another slice of French bread to her plate and handed the basket to Colbie as if nothing was out of the ordinary. "I'm mostly waiting for something from Brooke. We texted on Friday, and I'm hoping she's going to answer me back."

"Brooke's coming to visit for sure? Did she say?" Hope lifted in Lil's voice as she settled at the table. "I do hope she does. Such a dear girl. Terrible, what happened to her."

No one argued with that. Bree thought of her oldest half sister and the difficult hand she'd been dealt in life. The table silenced, as if she wasn't alone in her respect and hopes for Brooke.

"It would be hard for her to come at all," Colbie said gently, handing her mother the breadbasket. "I know the plan is that she wants to be here for Bree's trial, but then I think about what she has to be feeling. Sitting in another courtroom again would be doubly painful."

"I agree," Lil added. "Poor girl. It's God's goodness that she got through her hardship, but I don't think she's out of it entirely, even if she doesn't share that with us."

That was true, too. Bree took a sip of apple cider. "If she was coming, I would have heard by now."

"I know she wants to be here with you," Brandi sympathized. "Maybe she just can't."

"I don't want to bring up painful memories for her." She knew exactly what it was like to be haunted by images that would not let go. As she sliced into her serving of homemade lasagna, she was mindful of the trauma she had survived, and that it was much less than what others had endured. She hadn't been the one to die in that restaurant. Brooke had known injustice, Max saw tragedy day in and day out, and the courts were teeming with crime. Look at Lil, confined to a wheelchair.

She wanted to say it wasn't fair, but God didn't promise life was fair. Only that He stood for justice. It made it easier to put her worries in perspective.

Her cell binged, muffled by her sweater pocket. She took a bite of Lil's extraordinary lasagna and dug out her phone.

"Is it Brooke? No, I'm sure it's him," Colbie decided, apparently delighted. "We got off the subject of Max Decker. I think we had better get back onto it."

"Maybe it's Brooke," Lil wondered. "If it is her, Bree, tell her she is welcome to stay with us. I know she can't afford a hotel room."

"I'll tell her." She knew the text was from Max even before she glanced at the screen. Maybe because he had been on her mind, but then, he was always there.

Thinking of you, he had written. What R U up 2?

No good, she typed back. U?

"Oh, it *is* him." Lil vibrated with happiness. "Look at her. She's glowing."

"He has that affect on her," Brandi joyfully announced.

Her family. Bree blushed, because what was happening between her and Max felt intensely private. "We're only planning date number two, so don't start planning the wedding shower yet."

"I heard that." Lil trilled as she gathered up her knife and fork. "He's answered you already. You know what that means, don't you?"

"I'm afraid to hear whatever it is you're going to say." Bree took another bite of lasagna and risked a peek at the message waiting for her.

Marcus and I R going to a movie, he'd written. Wanna come?

"Ooh!" Colbie, leaning in her chair, caught sight of the screen. "He's asking her out again."

"Already?" Lil looked so ecstatic, she nearly dropped her forkful of salad.

"I *knew* it." Brandi pumped her fist in the air. "Yes!"

"I'm the one who is suppose to be excited." She loved her family. "Too bad I have to turn him down."

"Don't do that." Brandi's jaw dropped. "Don't."

"You should go with him." Colbie snatched the phone out of Bree's hands.

"Hey!" She tried to grab it back.

Colbie hopped off her chair. "What do you want me to say to him?"

"This isn't funny, Cole." Why was she laughing? Maybe because Lil's merry chuckle was such a happy sound. There was so little for her to find joy over these days. "Lil, tell your daughter to give me back my phone."

"Colbie, honey, Bree really should answer her own messages."

"No, she'll say no because she's here with us." Colbie, dear Colbie, all caring heart. Her motives were right. The question was, what would she say to Max?

"I don't feel right leaving you in the middle of dinner for a date."

"Invite him over!" Brandi suggested.

"He might not be far away," Colbie reasoned, her thumbs flying over the tiny keyboard. "I'll ask him."

"Why am I imagining disaster?" Bree almost got out of her chair to intercept, but the look on Colbie's face stopped her. Rare happiness sparkled in her navy blue eyes, and her smile was true and animated, a hint of the sister Colbie used to be before hard times hit. Impossible to take that away, she realized, and stayed in her chair. It was probably the only romance Colbie would be able to participate in for a long while.

"What are you saying, sweetheart?" Lil struggled to get her salad speared with her fork tines.

Bree leaned closer, guided the top handle of the fork, and helped her.

"Thank you, dear." There was nothing like the reward of Lil's smile. It could warm a person to the soul. Colbie was lucky to have her for a mom, hands down.

"I just asked him to come over if he hasn't had dinner." Colbie informed them, retaining possession of the phone as she took her chair. "Oh, he's answered already. He's coming."

"Praise the Lord!" Lil clasped her hands together, leaving her fork to clatter to her plate. "I've been praying so hard for my first son-in-law. Do you think this could be him?"

"You aren't the only one praying." Colbie returned the phone. "He said he was nearby, so he should be here in a few minutes."

"I'll get an extra plate." Brandi bounced up from her place across the table.

"Make it two." She tried to quiet her suddenly jumpy stomach. "He's bringing Marcus."

"Right." Brandi disappeared, practically sprinting.

"I adore that boy." Lil was talking on about how he'd charmed her at the bookstore. Colbie hopped up to draw two extra chairs up to the table.

Bree found herself scooting the table settings and food dishes around to make room for the plates Brandi brought from the kitchen. Everyone radiated joy.

Joy. That was a nice change of pace. But could it last? She'd learned happiness was a fleeting thing. Hoping it would be different this time, she pushed away from the table and went to the kitchen to heat more bread.

Max pulled to a stop next to Brianna's little blue car. "Mind your manners."

"I think I have some." Marcus seemed pretty chipper as he released his seat belt, as if he were getting a big kick out of watching his big brother sweat. "Not that it matters. I mean, it's not like you're serious about her."

"Yeah, I know you're giving me a hard time." He was way too serious about her. That was the problem. "Remember this. One day you might have a girlfriend, and think of how you want me to treat you."

"Uh, I'm getting a scary picture here, bro." Marcus opened the door. "I'm rethinking the hard time I was planning on giving you."

"I would have believed you meant it if you hadn't winked." He pocketed his keys and dropped to the ground. Typical trailer park. Not the best he'd seen, not the worst. He headed toward the gate to the faded white picket fence.

"You know I'm glad for you, right?" Marcus caught up to him.

"I know." He slapped his brother on the back, the closest he got to warm and fuzzy.

"Bree's cool. I think you should marry her."

"Marry her?" His foot caught on the concrete walkway, but it wasn't because commitment frightened him. The truth was, he wasn't afraid of much. Just one thing: losing Brianna.

"I know, not my business." Marcus pushed through the gate, loping with a teenage boy's awkward grace. "But I'm just saying. I would be in favor of it, you know. Just in case."

"I'll keep that in mind." He rolled his eyes, trying not to let his brother's well-meant comments trouble him. The door swung open and Brianna appeared, looking lovely as always. She was what he needed most.

"Hey, Bree!" Marcus loped up the switch-back wheelchair ramp instead of taking the adjacent steps. "Good to see you again. What is that delectable aroma?"

"Lasagna. It's Lil's recipe, but Colbie made it." She backed up to let him parade inside, his shirttails and unzipped coat trailing behind him. The rumble of his voice continued from inside the trailer, presumably talking to the other ladies.

Max could only pay attention to Bree. With her hair loose, she wore a gray MSU sweatshirt and worn Levis, and she had never looked more amazing. The sunlight brightened when she stepped out to greet him. The warm rays shined as if just for her. The love within him coiled ever tighter around his heart, cutting deep without a single shield to stop it. "It's good to see you, darlin'."

"Ditto." She stepped into his arms as she'd been longing to do so. He caught a glimpse of the dark circles under her eyes before her cheek came to rest against the plane of his chest.

She'd had a tough night, that was his guess. He held her tight, breathing in the scent of her strawberry-scented shampoo and wanting to take away her pain. Too vulnerable, that's what he was. He'd let her in too far. He had no clue what to do about that.

"Do you hear them in there?" She stepped away, just a step. Her long blond hair shimmered like gold, and serenity radiated from her, sweet and beautiful. "Don't get me wrong. I'm *so* glad you're here, but Lil and Colbie are especially excited. Please, you have to forgive them ahead of time."

"Forgive them for what?"

"You'll see." She held out her hand, slender and delicate.

Every fiber of his being, every thread stitching him together tugged excruciatingly—it was just the depth of his love for her. Cherishing her, he fit her hand to his. How good it was to be with her again. He felt her happiness at seeing him again; felt the sorrows pulling at her. Uncertain, not knowing how this would end, he let her lead him onto the narrow porch and through the front door.

"I hope you like lasagna," she said over her shoulder.

The moment his boots hit the green shag carpet, he was overwhelmed by the most delicious scents: spicy sauce, warm buttery bread and apple cider. Marcus was already at the table, grinning like a bear at a salmon buffet because he was being waited on by the other three women.

"Welcome, Max." Lil was dishing up a plate of salad for the boy. "What a blessing it is to have you over. It has been a long time since we've had such handsome men over to dine with us."

"And judging by the sorry fellows that just walked into your home, you will be waiting a little longer for those handsome men." Max shucked off his jacket, intensely aware of

Brianna at his side taking the garment from him. She moved with so much grace, it made his teeth ache. The simple act of laying a coat on the back of the nearby sofa dazzled him. She was everything he had ever dreamed of, down-to-earth sweetness and a golden heart. But with the way she looked at him…it was with need. The need for security, or for his love?

His stomach turned cold. He couldn't get her words out of his mind. *I always feel safe with you.* That's why Nancy had dated him in the first place. As he held Bree's chair for her and helped her scoot in to the table, he couldn't get past the similarities.

Tough childhood. Family of origin torn apart. A humble income. Working hard to better her life. A past trauma that had made the world feel unsafe. In Nancy's case, a former boyfriend and in Bree's the upcoming trial that made him a safe harbor in a turbulent sea.

"Sweet!" Marcus announced from the other side of the table, his head lifting from a silent blessing and dug in. "Thanks, Brandi. I can't remember the last time I ate anything this good."

"Eat up, then, young man." Lil preened, beaming with happiness at having a kid at the table, someone to mother. She tried lifting the pitcher of iced tea but couldn't budge it. Her hand and arm shook weakly.

"Let me." Brianna lifted the pitcher for her, leaning over her plate to fill the extra glass. "Lil, you haven't touched your lasagna."

"I've been too thrilled having you all here, dear." The older lady's faced wreathed with joy. Dark brown curls spilled over her light blue eyes as she gazed around the table, taking in the luxury, perhaps, of having so many visitors surrounding her. Trapped in a wheelchair, her life can't be easy, Max reflected, unable to stop the slide of deeper affection for Brianna, who set down the pitcher, nudged Marcus's glass toward him and loaded Lil's spoon with lasagna.

"I can do it, dear."

"I know, but I worry about you." This was Brianna revealed. Pure caring and concern. She wasn't using him, she wasn't intentionally turning to him the way Nancy had. But that didn't mean the outcome wouldn't be the same.

He did his best to put the brakes on his feelings, for all the good it did. The doubts did not stop, neither did his love for her.

"I worry about you, too, with all you have to face in the upcoming months." Meaning the trial. Lil patted Brianna's hand in reassurance.

"I'll be okay, don't you worry. Because I have all of you." She eased down next to him, smiling at everyone around the table, finishing with him. Pure adoration in that look, and he felt the honesty of it clear through.

She suddenly was too close and vulnerable, going through an exceptionally tough time, recovering from being a victim. He feared that was why she was drawn to him.

Colbie set a plate piled with food in front of him.

"Thanks. It smells incredible."

"You're welcome. Eat up."

Bree filled his glass with iced tea. Lil wanted him to get some salad, too, because he needed his greens. Brandi handed him a basket of buttered bread. Marcus winked at him, obviously loving the attention and the food.

This was everything missing in his life. Love, family, pleasant interaction. Colbie was talking about a Bible study, while Lil was asking Marcus about school. A quiet drop of longing filled him, the need for a life like this, a family of his own crowded around the dinner table.

"You look as if you're enjoying this." Bree leaned close, her words a pleasant brush against his ear.

"Very much." He didn't know how else to say it. He couldn't find the words to tell her, and especially not with so many people around. Bittersweet—finally finding exactly what he needed and at the same time suspecting it might not turn out to be his. She would recover, strengthen and might need a man very different from him.

When he bowed his head for a quick blessing, his prayers were for Brianna. For her happiness, for her to find what she needed in life.

Even if it was not him, in the end.

"I can't tell you what this means to me." Bree held the big bucket of buttered popcorn as Max settled into the chair beside her. The lights began to dim, she lost sight of the rest of the group farther down the row. The rumble of conversations in the mostly empty theater diminished. "Thanks for taking everyone out with us."

"No problem. I know how important your family is to you." He tucked the colas into the chairs' cup holders. "Besides, Lil looks like she's getting a kick out of all this."

"It's a treat for her." She couldn't help glancing down the aisle, where Brandi, Marcus and Colbie sat next to Lil in the reserved for wheelchairs section. They were sharing tubs of popcorn, courtesy of Max. "You're a good guy. You've gone two notches up in my estimation."

"Back at ya." He tore the wrapping off two straws, intent on the task. Something was missing. Somehow he felt more distant, as if he had taken a step back.

Was it her doubts making her feel that way? Throughout the evening, she'd watched him. He'd talked and laughed over the meal, he'd invited everyone to the family-rated movie as his treat, he'd helped Lil with her wheelchair and showed her sisters respect. Every moment, her love for him changed. It had doubled, impossibly larger and more important than it had been before.

She hadn't known love could do that. That it could keep transforming and expanding, taking you right along with it. Her feet were no longer on that mountain, but floating above it. As if she had hold of a helium balloon, a very tiny one, impossibly holding her up in the air.

The fall would be even more treacherous. If that didn't scare her enough, not falling was even more perilous. She felt trepidation shiver through her as he stretched his arm and settled it around her shoulders.

"Come closer," he whispered, his voice a beloved sound.

Why did love peel a person away in layers, one after another? Just when you thought you couldn't bear the exposure anymore, it went deeper. This wasn't like anything she'd known before. The fear of getting closer, the fear of failing had doubled, too. She felt every shadow within, every flaw. History seemed to murmur to her about her mother's chaotic relationships, Lil's sad one, her dad, his jail sentence and how he'd treated everyone he'd loved. Things that ran like a major earthquake fault through her life. Things he needed to understand first, before he could truly be in love with her.

"You can always lean on me. No matter what." He drew her nearer, a strong, good man who went beyond dreams. Who stood for what was right, who never faltered in the dark. When he'd been shot, he was not afraid of shadows, or of it happening again. Nothing rattled his world.

Trust this will work out, she told herself and rested her cheek against his steely shoulder. She loved being able to lean on him. "I appreciate your offer, but you might want to change your mind down the road."

"Why would you say that? Plan on leaving me for a better guy?" His tone came lightly, layered over seriousness.

"What better guy could there be?" She couldn't imagine one. He was like a prince out of a child's storybook, hewn of the right stuff.

"Says the storybook princess." He pressed a kiss to her forehead.

His tenderness made her eyes burn. She blinked, feeling as if the helium balloon she was holding on to had suddenly jerked her upward another thousand feet. "I'm no princess," she argued. "More like a pauper."

"You're perfection, Brianna."

Perfection? She was so far from it, it wasn't even funny.

He believed it. He gazed at her as if she were the most precious thing on earth to him. As if she were without flaws and a past, without imperfections or foibles. As if he would live and die for her.

No one had ever looked at her like that before. Her love for him doubled again, lifting her higher than she had ever been. Than she could ever feel comfortable being. What would happen when he began to see her differently, as she was?

A smart woman would stop this before she got hurt. Before she stopped defying gravity, the balloon popped and she fell back to solid ground, destroyed.

He's going to see the real you soon enough, a thought popped into her head. *What are you going to do until then?*

Hold on, she decided. As hard as it was to hope, as difficult as it was to let him closer, that's what she was going to do. She would not give in to fear. Nowhere on earth was as safe as being in his arms. He was her beloved, her chance for a fairy tale come true.

She would believe. Regardless how high the fall, she took the risk, opened the last door to her heart and snuggled more deeply against him.

As if he understood, he tightened his arms around her, holding on.

Chapter Fourteen

"My favorite part was when the dude jumped in the helicopter, figured out how to fly it and then chased the bad guys down the freeway." Marcus, in the truck's back seat, was at it again. The kid was a constant chatterbox. "Maybe instead of buying me a car one day, you could let me get a chopper."

"Sure, that's just what I'm gonna do." Wryly, he chanced a glance at the woman in the seat beside him. "I'm sorry about this. I thought it wouldn't be so bad if he tagged along. But you and I can't get a word in edgewise."

"I'm totally insulted." Bree bit her lip, trying not to laugh. "So much, that it's my treat next time. Maybe I could bring a movie over. Pop some corn."

"Max'll spring for the pizza." Marcus had no trouble volunteering him.

Probably because the kid knew he'd do anything for Brianna. She was a piece of his soul. When he wanted to reach out and lay his hand over hers, he kept his grip on the steering wheel. When he wanted to say, "name the day," he kept silent.

"Pepperoni, dude." Marcus was apparently thinking about food again. "We should do it this week. Whatcha think?"

"I can't this week." Brianna took a slow breath, as if she were gathering her courage. "I've got some stuff to deal with. My teaching practice sessions start at one of the grade schools."

"Cool. What about the weekend? It'll be like your third date, right? Hey, you don't mind if I hang out with you, do you?"

"I would miss you if you weren't there." Earnest, she twisted in her seat to add her smile.

"Sweet!"

"Glad to see you two have figured out my social life for me." He grinned. "Did either of you ask me if I was busy?"

"You aren't." Marcus answered for him. "He's never busy. Oh, that's my phone. I've got to get it. It's Ashleigh from the bookstore night."

"Your brother has a girlfriend?" she asked over the sound of Marcus answering his phone with a suave "Yo."

"He wishes, although I hope his prospects are good." Max slowed to take the turn into the trailer park. "You've gotten quiet. The kid might have been making a lot of noise, but I noticed."

"I figured. You kept glancing at me while you were driving." Night had fallen, and lights glowed in windows as they drove by.

"You worried about tomorrow?"

"I would be lying if I said I wasn't." She squared her shoulders. "I have a question for you."

"Sure."

"Do you think the reason love doesn't work out is because of a person's flaws?" She couldn't stand to see the realization dawn on his face, so she turned toward the window. Home after home flashed by, trees waved in the wind, and she felt her shadows. The face reflected back at her in the dark glass was more hollow than whole, and her pulse galloped in fast, thick beats as she waited for his answer. As she waited for him to realize she was speaking about herself.

"I think relationships fail for more important reasons." He thought of his own experience and of his parents'. "It's easy to grow apart. It's easy to want to love someone more than you actually do. To mistake security for love. To be wrong about what you want."

"And a person's flaws?"

"Why, have you started to notice a few more of mine?" His tone stayed light, but there was more she could not read. Where once he had been revealed to her, she could not feel his heart.

That is what is missing, she realized too late. The connection that bound them, the tie of affection between her soul and his was gone. As close as she was to him, she felt oddly alone.

"I think you are my knight in shining armor." Her voice cracked, proof of her stubborn love for him. "You've done so much for me without a thought for yourself. Look at tonight. I know what you've done."

"I'm guilty of taking you to a movie."

She did not know what emotions shaded his eyes and deepened the darkness around him, ones he tried to hide with a wink and a grin. She didn't know if she could hide her ever-increasing affection. "You took my family out, you made Lil happy, which has made both Colbie and Brandi happy. And me—"

"What about you?"

"I can count on you. That means the world to me."

"It is my pleasure." Sweet, sure, but there was more depth she could not see. He slowed down to turn onto the last street. "I know it's going to be a busy week for you, and you have school stuff going on, and the trial coming up after that. I meant what I said back in the theater. I'm here for you. No matter what."

"I know." There was the Max she knew, stalwart and amazing. But so distant. He could have been a stranger. She remembered the man she'd spotted in the bakery that night when Billy had been a no-show. She had marveled at Mr. Perfect, wondering what it would be like to feel his hand in hers, this man who at first impression was far out of her league.

He was even more now, and everything she had ever wanted. But there was so much he didn't know about her.

"You never answered my question." The words came haltingly and far too thin, laced with emotion and sadness. Sorrow, because she felt as if she were somehow losing a measure of closeness with him.

"I think flaws are different from faults." He stopped the truck in the gravel in front of the picket fence. "Faults are what can break a person or a relationship. Lying, cheating, pretending to be someone you're not."

"And flaws?" Her hand trembled as she released the seat belt. She hung on his answer, with both hope and reluctance. When it came to love, she did not know if blind faith was enough.

"There's someone sitting on the front porch. Do you recognize him?"

"What?" She glanced over the dash, peering through the dark windshield as headlights swept close, spotlighting the tall, too lean man who was rising, trying to see who had pulled up.

Dad. Bree went cold all the way to her soul. She blinked, part of her not wanting this to be true. The last time she'd heard news of him, he'd been asking Luke for money from an out-of-state federal prison. It couldn't be him. Not now, not when Max was here. It was too much.

"He looks like a vagrant." Max cut the engine and released his belt. "Let me deal with this. You stay here."

"No!" The word rang too sharp, and she winced, hearing the raw-edged panic. "It's no vagrant. Not officially, anyway."

"You know who that is?"

She nodded, not quite able to say the words. "I'm going to go talk to him before Colbie pulls up. This is going to upset Lil something terrible."

"No way am I going to let you talk to him alone. Not in the dark." Max had his door open and his feet on the ground before she could stop him.

Dad—Mick McKaslin—pushed open the

little gate, quite as if he owned the place. His time in jail had not been kind to him. His face was haggard and hollow, his hair thin and too long, gone gray. His clothes were wrinkled and too big for his frame. His grin came just as widely.

"Brandilyn! I thought that was you."

She slid down from the truck before Max could circle around and get the door for her. She caught his surprised glance. She and Brandi might look alike, but anyone who knew them got it right. Revealing.

"I'm Brianna." She was aware of Marcus hopping down behind her, coming to stand beside her. Max stood protectively between her and Mick, his feet braced, like a hero of old.

"Bree? Is that you? I never could tell the two of you apart." He flashed his grin, the one that made him look disarmingly like a good old guy, but it no longer worked with her.

"Max, this is my father." She drew in a sustaining breath, praying for courage before she said the words that would ruin everything between them. "He's apparently just finished serving a jail sentence for counterfeiting and fraud and a few other things."

Max's eyebrows shot up in surprise, and for a moment he looked as if he were about to speak, but he didn't. The night darkened, and when the wind gusted between them it carried an icy edge. The man she loved turned into a distant shadow, nothing more.

His voice sounded hollow when he finally spoke. "And you are just telling this right now?"

"I know." She bowed her head, not wanting to watch him retreat further.

"Good to meet you, Max, is it?" Mick stuck out his hand, as if he didn't have a thing to be ashamed of. As if he were a reformed man. She thought of all the times he'd been reformed, and born again. More times than was believable in any man's lifetime. "Who is that pulling up? Is that my little Colbie?"

Bree thought of Lil in the car, and how hurt she was going to be at having to see Mick again. "Max, it would be best if you left. You and Marcus don't want to be part of this."

"I can take a little trouble." His hand caught hers. "Do you need my help?"

She couldn't stand the spark of emotion zinging from his touch. The understanding concern of his tone made her feel an inch tall. I'm not like Nancy, she wanted to tell him, but she had lied. By omission, sure, but it was still a lie. Ashamed, she withdrew her hand and her heart. "No, I'll be fine without you, Max. Go ahead and go."

In the background she realized Brandi was

getting out of Colbie's car, hands fisted, jaw set, defensive.

"Brandi, it's good to see you." Dad jovially turned toward her. "I would know you anywhere. How have you been, baby girl?"

The shame spread like poison ivy, itchy and burning and unbearable. Max was turning away, appearing torn. When he held out his hand, she couldn't take it. All that he offered—love, trust, dreams—how could she reach for them now? The lie of omission stood between them, maybe too much like the story he'd told her about Nancy. Lil's outcry of alarm and anguish stained the beautiful night. Dad's pleasant, "Lil, I'm crushed you don't want me here," was proof that she could not escape her past.

"Come walk me to my truck." Max's hand waited for hers, palm up, trembling a little, an invitation of everything she longed for.

Dad and Colbie were arguing now, anger growing fiercer until it drowned out Lil's sobs.

"I can't." This chaos was just the start of things. The upset Dad could cause within a few minutes of saying hello would be getting worse any minute. "Go, before—"

"Bree, that nice young man of yours has quite a truck there. He must have money. Think he can float me a loan for just a few days? I—"

"That's it." She grabbed Max by the elbow and pulled all two hundred pounds of him toward his open door. "You have to go. I can't imagine why you aren't running away from me."

"Bree, I don't know what's going on here but—"

"Go." She couldn't look at him. She was that little girl standing in the living room while Brandi cried inconsolably, listening to their parents fighting in the kitchen. The crash of a beer bottle. The shattering wine glass. The overdue bills unpaid and no food in the cupboards. She was the little girl with shoes from the charity store at church, and the state-sponsored school lunches. The girl too ashamed to go to school the entire week after her Dad was caught shoplifting at their small-town grocery store. The past came crashing back, when she felt least able to fight it. And now Max would know.

"Goodbye." She turned her back on him so he wouldn't see the tears fall. Every breath cracked her into pieces. Every second that passed was like slowly dying until his truck turned over and the cab lights flared on.

"Brianna." His baritone fell low, hard to hear over the idling engine. "Why didn't you tell me?"

His question told her everything she needed

to know. She was simply another woman who had lied to him. Another woman who could bring ugliness into his life.

How could she answer his question? She couldn't tell him the truth. How did she explain she wanted the life beyond the fairy tale so very badly? That she had tricked herself into hoping that a good life well lived, full of love and caring family could be meant for her.

"Why aren't you leaning on me?" he asked.

She couldn't answer. Aching for what she did not have, for what she was afraid she could never find, she prayed for him to go. Relief filled her when she heard him put his truck in gear and slowly backed into the road. Surely he saw it, too—that she was not the perfect princess he'd made her out to be. It didn't matter that she'd tried to tell him. She knew without him saying so that it was over. He couldn't love her now.

Devastation wrapped like a lead blanket around her. She'd known from the first time she'd laid eyes on him that he couldn't be meant for her.

As if to prove his honor, Max pulled closer to the argument and hopped back out of his truck. He must have gotten his badge out of his glove box, because after he stopped to speak to Lil, he flashed it at her dad. Colbie was rigid with anger, Brandi was crying. Bree closed her eyes so she wouldn't watch the man she loved escort her father to his truck.

"Max's great. He's taking Dad away." Brandi rushed to her side. "Can you believe he came here?"

"I can believe anything." She could hold the tears inside. Really, she could. She listened to the truck's engine fade into the night. She couldn't seem to take her gaze from the darkness, as if waiting for Max to drive back down the road, as if he might change his mind. As if he wanted to tell her he could not live without her, in spite of everything she was.

Not happening, Bree. Odds were that he would never think of her as a storybook princess again. She blinked hard against the strange blurring of her vision—it *was* blurring, not tears—and was grateful when Brandi took her by the hand.

"C'mon. Lil's pretty upset. She needs all the comfort we can give her."

"Right." Her feet were disconnected from the rest of her, but somehow she got them to move her forward. The metaphoric balloon she'd been dangling from popped, and she hit the ground so hard, her soul shattered.

"Do you think Max will understand about Dad?" Brandi asked.

"Would you?"

"No." Her twin's voice sounded very small, aware of the truth neither of them could say.

Max was a great guy. But maybe as fantastic as he was and as thoroughly as she'd fallen in love with him, he wasn't *the* guy. Maybe he wasn't her man. Sometimes you didn't get what you wanted. Sometimes the girl didn't get her hero. There weren't enough happy endings to go around. Life was proof enough of that.

They fell silent, afraid to say what they were both thinking. That girls like them didn't have the chance for happy-ever-afters. She had asked God the same question over and over again. *I'm not destined to be alone, right, Lord?*

Tonight, she'd received her answer.

"Do you think that's him?" Brandi asked in the dark confines of the passenger seat as the phone began to ring. They were driving home, too late for Brianna's comfort. "Want me to see who's calling?"

"No." Her fingers tightened on the wheel.

"What if it's Max? He might want to talk to you."

"Are you kidding? He drove off with Dad. He's spent time with him. There's no way he's going to want to talk to me now."

Brandi bowed her head, falling silent, unable to disagree.

Yes, it was truly good and over with Max.

She stopped for a red light, waiting as no other cars crossed the intersection. The rumble of the engine and the whir of the heater sounded loud in the silence. She knew Brandi wanted to talk about what happened, to somehow try to change the outcome. But there was no changing the truth. This relationship had never been going to work out, not really. He was always going to figure out that the way he wanted to see her and the way she was were two entirely different things.

Although losing him did hurt more than anything she'd encountered yet in life.

The light flicked to green and she checked both ways before pulling out, motoring up to the twenty-five-mile-an-hour speed limit. For the first time ever she felt drained and empty, without hope. She had never realized before all the little ways hope had crept into her life like tendrils of roots clinging to the earth, determined to grow. How she always looked to the future and to God for something better.

Like a little girl clutching to her books of fairy tales, dreaming of a castle and true love instead of an unkempt trailer and parents passed out in the next room. How she had to believe that God meant something better for her and Brandi. That belief had gotten her through her childhood and through fighting for her life in I.C.U.

And now that was gone. She had a clear view of her future without Max. Grief scored through her more painfully than any bullet. She hadn't realized her hopes had gotten so big. She'd let herself imagine—just a little—what life could be like spent at his side, in his arms, in his heart. She could picture a proposal with him on bended knee, a wedding with yellow roses and a long white gown, and every day privileged to see Max's lopsided grin, laugh at his wry humor and stand tall with him through good times and bad.

Not gonna happen, Bree. Forget it.

But those wishes had obstinately burrowed into the tenderest places of her soul. Everything she was ached for those impossible dreams. Dreams she could never have. Her eyes burned, and she focused on the street in front of her. The yellow and black lines rushing in front of the car guided her home. When those lines blurred, she blinked hard and brought them back into focus.

The phone chimed, signaling a text message, the tone muffled by the confines of her handbag.

"I'm going to see who that is." Brandi

leaned forward against the seat belt to unzip the bag. "Dad wouldn't leave a text. He doesn't have a phone."

"Please, don't." A few raindrops speckled the windshield, making it harder to see. She felt like the night, desolate and cold, starless with a storm moving in. "There's no way Max is going to forgive me."

"Forgive you? Wait, I don't get it." She didn't stop digging around until she came up with the cell. She cradled it in her hand, as if debating. "I thought this is about Dad."

"It is." All the feeling drained out of her. Numbness set in, the same way it had after she'd been shot. For a brief moment, she'd felt nothing. Her system was too shocked. When her brain caught up with her nerve endings, she was going to be in horrible pain. "Either that message is him rejecting me, or he wants to get together face-to-face to do it."

"He's a really great guy. He's a lot to lose."

Bree nodded, her throat closing up. He was everything. Last time she'd hurt like this, she'd been in I.C.U.

The phone chimed again.

"Don't get that, Brandi. Please." She nudged on her turn signal and turned onto their street.

"But it's from him. Can I at least see what he said?"

"No." She answered too late. Her twin had already punched through the scroll list to open a message.

Brace yourself for another emotional bullet, Bree. She pulled up every shield she had, every defense around her battered heart. How could it be enough? She loved him so truly, there was no protection. No refuge. Not even now.

"Don't tell me what it says." She slowed as rain began to fall in earnest, obscuring the stretch of the street in front of her. It was like driving into the worst darkness without a light to guide her way. "I'm better off not knowing how badly I messed this up."

"This is Dad's fault, not yours. He's supposed to be in jail. How could they let him out on parole?" Brandi fell silent, studying whatever was on the screen. "Do you know what Max sent?"

"I told you, no. I don't want to hear it. I already know." Rain battered the windshield, and her spirit felt the cold hard strikes. She spotted a white pickup parked along the curb in front of their duplex, and the shock wore off. Endless grief tunneled through her, leaving her weak. Shakily, she turned into the driveway, looking straight ahead, grateful for the dark that hid him from her sight. For the dark that hid the tears in her eyes.

There was no hope left. No one speck within her. All the years of her life, she had managed to grasp tightly to it no matter what. The blows in her life simply had not been hard enough break her hold. But the realization that Max was never going to really love her, that it couldn't be her future was the biggest blow she'd ever taken.

"He sent a chapter and a verse." Why wasn't Brandi giving up? She had to have spotted the truck. She knew Max was here.

"Hebrews 11:1. You know that verse. It's one of your favorites."

The car crept into the utter darkness beneath the carport, the beating rain deafening. Bree turned off the motor, wishing she could turn off her feelings as easily. But they crashed through her like a tidal wave hitting the shore, obliterating everything, knocking down and dragging the pieces of her shattered hope out to sea. There was no way to get them back. They were forever lost, never to be found and made whole again.

"Now faith is being sure of what we hope for and certain of what we do not see," Brandi quoted as Max stepped out of the dark.

Chapter Fifteen

Seeing her again brought it all back. How Brianna had hid the truth about her dad. Of her standing with her back to him, her head bowed, her slender shoulders trembling, closing him out. Rain drenched him, and the night's chill had crept deep beyond the skin. Cold and hollow, he approached her car, waiting for her to come out and face him.

Her window zipped down, revealing her. She was little more than a shadow in the confines of the car, her features as hidden to him as her feelings.

"I took your Dad to the Y." He winced at how terse he sounded, harsher than he'd meant. "That was about all he could afford."

"I hope he didn't try to get you to loan him money. He's not good for it." She was cold as the night, as impenetrable as the shadows. Impossible to know what she was feeling. If she was going to reject him again or hear him out.

"He tried, but I had the man figured out." He jammed his hands in his pockets. Rain hammered the roof overhead, echoing in the confines of the carport, reminding him of a certain night long ago. Sweat broke out on the back of his neck. Tingles shot like fear into his bloodstream. "I deal with people like that all the time."

"Yes, I know." He'd never heard a deeper note of sadness. The door opened, and she slowly stood like someone gravely ill. She leaned heavily on the door. She took forever to straighten. Cloaked in shadows, all he could see was the hint of her profile and the dark pools of her eyes.

"I'm sorry. I should have told you about him—Dad." She stayed where she was, gripping the car door. She seemed so distant, she was like a stranger. "Back when you told me about Nancy, I should have opened those memories I keep closed and told you."

"I have eyes. I saw what happened tonight. He couldn't tell you and Brandi apart. Colbie's upset. Lil's tears. You all have been through so much because of that man."

"That you understand is all the proof I need. You are too good, Max. You've come here to let me down easy. I know this because—" She hiccupped, but he suspected it was a sob she tried to disguise. "Because you try to do the right thing. You're that man. You are going to end this the correct way. But I don't need that. What I need is for you to have mercy and walk away."

He'd been battling hurt and doubt all the way downtown, with Mick trying to buddy up to him and Marcus chattering on the phone in the backseat. She'd turned away from him, and that hurt. "You and I have differences, Bree."

"Too many. I'm glad you see it, too. It's one of the reasons I don't think about Dad. Don't you see?" She released her hold on the door and gave it a push. The thud resounded against the concrete and the walls of the house, flashing up memories he couldn't seem to stop.

"You haven't seen me at all, Max. Until tonight." She took a step closer, but her voice began to sound far away, tinny and echoing over the sound of the rain in his memory drumming harder, muffling a crack of thunder. "That girl you saw when you looked at me, the way you looked at me. You made me believe, too. Deep down, I knew better, which makes this all my fault. So you can go, guilt free. You're off the hook."

Her words registered, but what he also heard

was a revolver's report. The rush of the paramedics, their rubber-soled shoes splashing on the cement, and the strobing flash of sirens. He felt again the terror of telling his body to get up off the ground and finding himself still flat on his belly, unable to move anything but his right hand. The deadening whirlpool of betrayal had sucked him down. He'd lost his ability to truly trust in anyone. He didn't know how to get it back.

This was his out. She was giving him the chance to walk away without fault. He could go back to his life, raising Marcus, being a cop, studying his Bible and living without ever having to risk his heart again. He could hold up this moment as the badge of honor. I loved her, but she was at fault. She kept truths from me. She wasn't right for me. She was recovering from a serious trauma and I couldn't trust her to know what she wanted.

So easy to take that first step back into safety. Simple to let the darkness and the fear win. He would never have to open the last door into his heart. Never have to take down the final barrier where no one but God had been. He would never risk hurting the way he'd been hurt tonight again.

"I'm not guilt free in this." He set his shoulders and steeled his spine. "This is hard for a man like me to admit, but I got scared."

"Of the trouble my dad can cause, sure." She awkwardly buttoned her coat, taking a few steps in his direction. The tap of her step rang with uncertainty, but it brought her within reach of the security lights at the end of the carport. Illumination found her, revealing the tears shining in her eyes. Her sorrow held luster that rendered him speechless. Light sifted over her like tiny blessings and wishes come true.

Believe, a voice told him from down deep inside.

How could he? He wanted to. That's why he had come here. But it was as if he'd hit a wall, an impossible barrier he could not scale.

"There's something I need to know. Something I've always wondered about you." He gathered his courage. "You said something about the robbery that stuck with me. You said you went on with your life, regardless of how hard it was. You wouldn't let what happened stop you. That you wouldn't let them win. How did you do it? I've lost sight of almost everything I used to believe in."

"Like what?"

"Hope. Happy-ever-afters. That the good guy has a chance."

"That sounds like a lot to lose sight of." Her voice resonated with understanding. "I feel that way, too, right now, so I don't think I can help you."

Last time he had let belief take him over, he'd been blindsided. He saw now that he had never recovered. He was stuck on that rain-slicked driveway, and he'd never gotten up off it. He'd never done what Brianna had, climbed back on her feet and fought to keep on living wholly, open to all the goodness life has to give.

"How?" he asked.

"Job 2:10." She set her chin, fisted her hands and seemed so small even with the light tumbling over her. *"Shall we indeed accept good from God, and shall we not accept adversity?"*

"My faith in God is one thing that has survived." That was the honest truth. He felt captivated as she took another step closer.

"2 Corinthians 12:10. *Since I know it is all for Christ's good, I am quite content with my weaknesses and with insults, hardships, persecutions, and calamities. For when I am weak, then I am strong."*

Emotion burned behind his eyes and lodged like a hot, tight ball behind his ribs. He had been right in coming, right in following his heart. Brianna was good to the core, gentle to a fault. She had strength that awed him. Her radiance touched him deep and did not let go.

Unbearable love overwhelmed him. An emotion stronger than any force in the universe came softly, delicately, like spring unfurling the season's first blossom. The impenetrable, final steel wall within him melted like warm butter.

He believed. True love changed his world like a fairy tale; but it was no fictional story, no moment of make believe. God is love, he knew, as he felt a reassuring touch. Even a man like him deserved a happy ending and someone he could believe in.

"You are the most incredible woman." His hand cupped the side of her face, lovingly. "Even when I think I've got you figured out, you surprise me again. You have made me come alive, Brianna, in ways I didn't know I could."

"I don't understand." Her violet eyes filled with pure pain. "Didn't we both agree this isn't going to work?"

"I never agreed to that." Gentle, his words. Adoring, his tone. "I said we have differences. Who doesn't? What we share in common is more important. I need you, Bree. I love you."

"What did you say?" She jerked from his touch, shaking her head. She could *not* have heard him right.

"I love you, Brianna. From the bottom of

my heart. With all I am. With all I have." He cupped her face in both hands, gazing intently into her eyes as if in challenge, as if to prove the truth.

"But I should have told you the truth."

"I don't think you meant to deceive me, Bree. I think it was too painful of a subject to talk about with someone you were just starting to date."

"Yes." That was it exactly. "I'm not Nancy. I'm not using you. I would never hurt you."

"I know that, darlin'." His tone rumbled low, impossibly tender.

"But what about my dad?" She felt as if she were breaking apart from the inside out, one tiny piece at a time. "I've tried, but I can't escape my past and where I've come from. It's part of me."

"I know the answer to that, and I learned it from you. Don't look back at the bad stuff. Choose what you want to take with you from the good things in your past and keep moving forward." He did not remove his hands, his touch searing like a brand. He searched her face as if trying to see inside, where she could not let him go. "That's why I'm here tonight. I've come to ask you to move forward with me."

"Move forward?" Was he talking about

moving on? And why was he towering over her with his dark hair dusted with light and close enough to kiss her? "I don't understand at all. You want to break up."

"No way, beautiful." His voice vibrated pleasantly through her, a coziness like nothing she had known before. "We have to stay together."

"We don't." She wanted to pull way, but she couldn't move. "I can't go through this again, Max. My heart broke utterly. Totally. There's nothing left of it. I can't let myself hope. I can't let myself go through that again, needing you so much and then losing you again."

"Now see, we have that in common, too." The fury of the rain lessened, as if sensing the world was suddenly not quite as bleak. "I learned one thing tonight. I don't want to live without you. I can't be without you. My life would be empty, my days spent existing instead of living. I need you, Bree. I love you." He brushed his lips across her forehead. "Yes, I said I love you, my beautiful, strong Brianna."

"Right there is proof this can't work." His amazing words were cruel: everything she wanted; everything she could not have. "There you go again, seeing someone who isn't me."

"Oh, I see you. When I look at you, I see everything." His reverent tone was like the sweetest assurance, the brush of his lips to the tip of her nose the purest caress. "I see a woman who has pulled herself up by her bootstraps. Who does well in school, who loves her family, who handles adversity with grace and strength. She treats everyone with kindness and is true beauty, inside and out. This is what true love is, Brianna. Seeing the best in someone, and cherishing that above all else."

Tears seared her, burning behind her eyes and tangling behind her larynx. She didn't trust her voice. She didn't know what to do with his sweet words. Trust in them? She wasn't that naive. She could no longer let herself believe, didn't know if she could. She had no hope left. Every piece, every sliver was gone, as if washed away, no longer within her. When she needed it most.

"I have to work late some nights. Whenever my pager goes off, I have to drop whatever I'm doing and answer the call." He kept chipping away with his words and his outpouring of tenderness. "I leave my wet towels on the bathroom floor. I get caught up in sports shows and forget what day it is. And that's just the start of it. Can you accept these thing about me?"

"Yes." What was happening to her? Her ribs felt as if they were breaking, her entire being as if tearing apart. "I'm scared of the dark. I have post-traumatic stress. I double check every lock on every door every time."

"Flaws are what makes a person lovable." In the darkness he brushed his thumb over the cut of her bottom lip, the most tender of gestures. His gaze softened, as if he were about to kiss her again. As if he could breach the distance that had fallen between them. "Flaws are the dear things that make someone unique. One of a kind. Impossible to replace."

"Am I those things to you?"

"Absolutely, beyond a doubt, yes." His loving sincerity sucked all the sense from her brain and obliterating the entire world. The rain silenced. The cold night vanished. She stood as if in summer sunshine as his calloused fingertips gently scraped against her lower lip. The briefest stroke, but it held her captive. "Bree, you are what I never thought was possible. You are my one true love."

Hope should be lifting her up, but her feet were solidly planted on the ground. Maybe it was too late for them. Maybe her heart had been broken too much. His touch was warm comfort, but nothing more. There was no zing of emotion binding them together. No unspoken understanding as soul mates should share.

What had happened? Had she lost him? And how, when he was saying everything right, as if out of her dreams?

"I'm waiting for the words, Bree."

She laid her hands on his, feeling the rugged texture of his male skin and something vulnerable behind the strength and steel. Tiny pain needled deep within, as if what was left of her wishes were struggling to live.

Believe, her soul whispered. Just believe.

"Do you love me?" he asked with amazing tenderness. He dominated her senses; he seemed to shrink the night, his endless affection was all she could see.

"Yes," she answered, as if standing in full light. It was hard to make herself vulnerable one more time. "So much, I could never stop loving you."

"That's how I love you, too." A reverent grin stretched his dimples into full bloom.

Unable to move, totally captivated, she could only watch as he bent closer, bringing with him the scent of March rain and aftershave. His lips met hers in a sweet, velvet caress. Unstoppable love filled her soul with enough power to chase away every shadow and fear. As she clung to him, emotion snapped between them like an electric shock, binding them heart to heart.

She rested her cheek on his chest, savoring

the reliable beat of his heart and the shelter of his arms enclosing her. She could not believe that she was here with him, her soul mate—but it was true. How could she ever thank God enough for answering her most sincere prayer?

"It's stopped raining." Max kissed the top of her head, his happiness washing over her. "It's a good sign."

"It's like God answering." Moonlight spilled between parting storm clouds, silvering the world, gracing it with pearled light. The radiance touched her, filling her with hope for the future. Life was not perfect, but God was. Whatever happened on the road ahead, she knew she would be loved.

Just like the stories she held so dear, she had her happily-ever-after. She wrapped her arms around Max, thankful for him, and held on tight.

Epilogue

Three weeks later

At the sound of the electronic chime coming from the depths of her handbag, Bree tugged her phone out of her purse to check her messages. Sure enough, there was one just in from the man she was supposed to be meeting. She tapped the select button. Waiting for the text to flash onto her screen, she caught sight of Brandi whisking through the bakery's main aisle, balancing a tray of drinks and dessert.

I'm on my way, Max had written. Luv U much.

Luv U more, she typed with a smile because she knew that wherever he was, he was thinking of her.

Her phone chimed with a new message.

No, I luv U more, he argued.

Typical Max, always wanting the last word. Not that she minded, because being adored by him was the best blessing she'd ever received. She intended to cherish him for the rest of her life.

The front door chimed, and she twisted around, already knowing it wasn't him. Colbie wrestled with the door, and before Bree could hop up to go help, an older man rose from a nearby table to hold it. Lil offered a sweet note of thanks as Colbie wheeled her through the threshold.

"I had a hankering for banana muffins," Lil explained with an extra twinkle of happiness in her beautiful blue eyes. "Colbie was good enough to drive me here. You are looking especially lovely today. Happiness looks good on you, child."

"My practice teaching at the grade school has been totally fantastic." She got up to rearrange the chairs to make room for Lil's wheelchair. "Come, sit with me and tell me why you're so chipper."

"You know, the same old." Lil's smile couldn't be any bigger. What was going on?

"We don't want to interrupt," Colbie explained as she pushed her mother toward the counter. "Are you waiting for Max?"

"He's on his way. We're going to dinner afterward. Do you two want to join us?"

"Let's wait and see how the afternoon turns out." It was Colbie's turn to smile as if she had just heard the best news in the world. "We're going to order."

What was with those two? Honestly, she was glad they were happy, but she was clueless as to why. A girl liked to get the whole scoop. Bree settled back into her chair when the door opened again with a merry jingle. Out of the corner of her eye she caught sight of a lean woman with a battered duffel bag moving through the doorway. There was something familiar about the fragile cut of her shoulders. The tentative posture. The hint of a profile so like Colbie's. Big blue eyes, straight brown hair, and a heart-shaped face. Brooke.

"It's Brooke!" Colbie shrieked, streaking through the rows of tables to wrap their wayward sister in a hug.

"Brooke!" Brandi, her tray empty, raced over to join in. "I can't believe it. You came."

Bree didn't remember how she crossed the room, only that her sisters made room for her as she squeezed into the hug. Joy bubbled through her as she held Brooke tight. "It's good you're here."

"I'm so glad to see you all." Tears hovered but did not fall. Brooke looked changed; the years had not been kind to her. Bree ached for her sister, vowing to pray even harder for her happiness. After all, if the fairy tale could happen to her, it could happen to Brooke, too. No one deserved it more.

"I'm not late, am I?" She looked worried. "I came straight from the bus depot."

"Of course you're not late," Bree answered, pulling her car keys from her pocket. "The trial doesn't start for weeks. Did you want to stow your duffel in my car?"

"Thanks." When Brooke took the key ring, she glanced at Brianna's left hand. Relief washed across her face. "I'll take care of this bag after we catch up. Hi, Lil."

"Hi, dear. I'm thrilled you decided to come and visit us. Give me a hug, poor girl. You're looking much too thin." Lil held out her frail arms. "You must stay with us so I can fatten you up with some of our home cooking. No arguments."

"I've missed you all so much." Brooke's bottom lip trembled, and no one watching missed the brief flash of misery on her face, proof of what they all feared, that her life was much harder than she admitted. Maybe they could convince her to finally move home. She bent to accept Lil's welcoming hug.

The door chime knelled a third time, and Bree didn't need to look to know it was Max.

Her spirit turned toward him like the moon toward the earth, and her soul smiled. He dominated her view with his mile-wide shoulders and his windblown, dark hair spilling over his forehead. He was like her very own dream in a black bomber jacket, a day's growth shadowing his square jaw and striding directly toward her like a panther stalking his prey.

Tenderness for him blinded her to all else, so it took her a moment to realize he was not alone. She blinked, trying to bring Marcus and the strapping men with him into focus. Her half brothers had hung back, one with his hands in his pockets, the other with his arms folded in front of his chest, both watching her with impossibly blue eyes.

"Hunter? Luke?" She stared in surprise. The McKaslin boys didn't get the chance to visit much, since running the ranch kept them busy nearly 24/7. "What are you all doing here? I—" She fell silent realizing her entire family—those she counted as real family— were surrounding her and that Max had gone down on bended knee.

The entire bakery silenced, as if every single person there knew what he was about to ask.

"Brianna?" He gathered her hands respectfully in his.

Her pulse screeched to a halt. She stared

down at him in disbelief. He couldn't be proposing, could he? Joy popped like fireworks on the Fourth of July.

"Will you do me the honor of becoming my wife?" He slid a square-cut diamond ring on her finger, his gaze luminous, his adoration for her unquestionable.

"Yes. Of course. I would love to marry you." Endless love for him lifted her off the floor, or at least it felt that way as he wrapped her in his arms and gave her a perfect kiss.

While her family cheered, clapped and called out their congratulations, Brianna could see her future as Max's wife. With every day happier than the next, spent with her beloved, basking in his love. There would be children one day—maybe a little boy and a little girl— and more happiness and more love to share.

"It's going to be a good life," Max promised.

"It's going to be spectacular." Full of endless hope, she kissed her fiancé one more time, absolutely sure. The best was yet to come.

* * * * *

Dear Reader,

You may remember meeting Brianna and her twin, Brandilyn, in earlier books of THE MCKASLIN CLAN series, when they were teenagers dealing with their troubled lives. Time has passed; Brianna has grown up, and when I started writing her story, I realized trouble had found its way into her life again. The past was holding her back from the peace and joy God intended for her, I was curious. Could she heal the places in her spirit that had been hurt by violence and fear? Could she find a way to leave a childhood full of neglect and chaos behind her? And how?

When I first met Max Decker, I thought his steely outside, tender inside would be just what Brianna needed. Someone who was strong enough to always stand for what was right, but who could love her the way she deserved. I hope you enjoy reading about their journey toward love and hope and God's purpose for them.

Thank you for choosing *BLIND-DATE BRIDE*.

Wishing you love, hope and peace,

Jillian Hart

QUESTIONS FOR DISCUSSION

1. At the beginning of the story, how would you describe Bree's character? What are her weaknesses and her strengths? How has her past influenced who she is?

2. What strikes you most about Max's character when you first meet him? How does he change through the story?

3. Bree wonders why she couldn't have met Max before the robbery, before she had even more problems. She worries that love only happens when a person has worked out all her problems and flaws. What does this say about her? And why is she wrong?

4. How does Max's brother influence the story? What aspects of Max's character does Marcus bring out?

5. Bree is struggling with fear and trust issues. How does God lead her through? Have you ever struggled with similar issues?

6. Trauma had affected both Max and Bree. In what ways? Both Max and Bree say in the

story that violence has changed who they are. How is this true? In what ways do they begin to heal? Has this ever happened to you?

7. How does Bree rely on Scripture to strengthen her? How do you rely on Scripture to strengthen you?

8. In the course of the story, Bree makes the statement: The only way out of hardship and pain is to go straight through it. How does she do this? Have you had hardship you have had to work through in a similar way?

9. Bree struggles with letting Max close to her emotionally. How is this evident? What do you think are the underlying causes and issues?

10. What do you think are the important themes in this story?

11. How does the Lord lead Bree? How does He lead Max?

12. How would you describe Bree's faith? Max's faith? How are each strengthened?

13. What does Bree learn about flaws and about love?

14. How does joy and comfort come into Bree's and her sisters' lives? To Max's and Marcus's?

When her neighbor proposes a "practical" marriage, romantic Rene Mitchell throws the ring in his face. Fleeing Texas for Montana, Rene rides with trucker Clay Preston—and rescues an expectant mother stranded in a snowstorm. Clay doesn't believe in romance, but can Rene change his mind?

*Turn the page for a sneak preview of
"A Dry Creek Wedding"
by Janet Tronstad,
one of the heartwarming stories about
wedded bliss in the new collection
SMALL-TOWN BRIDES.
Available in June 2009 from Love Inspired®.*

"Never let your man go off by himself in a snowstorm," Mandy said. The inside of the truck's cab was dark except for a small light on the ceiling. "I should have stopped my Davy."

"I doubt you could have," Rene said as she opened her left arm to hug the young woman. "Not if he thought you needed help. Here, put your head on me. You may as well stretch out as much as you can until Clay gets back."

Mandy put her head on Rene's shoulder. "He's going to marry you some day, you know."

"Who?" Rene adjusted the blankets as Mandy stretched out her legs.

"A rodeo man would make a good husband," Mandy muttered as she turned slightly and arched her back.

"Clay? He doesn't even believe in love."

Well, that got Mandy's attention, Rene thought, as the younger woman looked up at her and frowned. "Really?"

Rene nodded.

"Well, you have to have love," Mandy said firmly. "Even my Davy says he loves me. It's important."

"I know." Rene wondered how her life had ever gotten so turned around. A few days ago she thought Trace was her destiny and now she was kissing a man who would rather order up a wife from some catalogue than actually fall in love. She'd felt the kiss he'd given her more deeply than she should, too. Which meant she needed to get back on track.

"I'm going to make a list," Rene said. "Of all the things I need in a husband. That's how I'll know when I find the right one."

Mandy drew in her breath. "I can help. For you, not for me. I want my Davy."

Rene looked out the side window and saw that the light was coming back to the truck. She motioned for Mandy to sit up again. She doubted Clay had found Mandy's boyfriend. She'd have to keep the young woman distracted for a little bit longer.

Clay took his hat off before he opened the door to his truck. Then he brushed his coat before climbing inside. He didn't want to scatter snow all over the women.

"Did you see him?" Mandy asked quietly from the middle of the seat.

Clay shook his head. "I'll need to come back."

"But—" Mandy protested until another pain caught her and she drew in her breath.

"It won't take long to get you to Dry Creek," Clay said as he started his truck. "Then I can come back and look some more."

Clay didn't like leaving the man out there any more than Mandy did, but it could take hours to find him, and the sooner they got Mandy comfortable and relaxed, the sooner those labor pains of hers would go away.

"I feel a lot better," Mandy said. "If you'd just go back and look some more, I'll be fine."

Clay looked at the young woman as she bit her bottom lip. Mandy was in obvious pain regardless of what she said. "You're not fine, and there's no use pretending."

Mandy gasped, half in indignation this time.

Those pains worried him, but he assumed she must know the difference between the ones she was having and ones that signaled the baby was coming. Women went to class for that kind of thing these days. She probably just needed to lie down somewhere and put her feet up.

"He's right," Rene said as she put her hand on Mandy's stomach. "Davy wouldn't want you out here. He'll tell you that when we find him. And think of the baby."

Mandy turned to look at Rene and then looked back at Clay.

"You promise you'll come back?" Mandy asked. "Right away?"

"You have my word," Clay said as he started to back up the truck.

"That should be on your list," Mandy said as she looked up at Rene. "Number one—he needs to keep his word."

Clay wondered if the two women were still talking about the baby Mandy was having. It seemed a bit premature to worry about the little guy's character, but he was glad to see that the young woman had something to occupy her mind. Maybe she had plans for her baby to grow up to be president or something.

"I don't know," Rene muttered. "We can talk about it later."

"We've got some time," Clay said. "It'll take us fifteen minutes at least to get to Dry Creek. You may as well make your list."

Mandy shifted on the seat again. "So, you think trust is important in a husband?"

"A *husband?*" Clay almost missed the turn. "You're making a list for a husband?"

"Well, not for me," Mandy said patiently. "It's Rene's list, of course."

Clay grunted. Of course.

"He should be handsome, too," Mandy added

as she stretched. "But maybe not smooth, if you know what I mean. Rugged, like a man, but nice."

Clay could feel Mandy's eyes on him.

"I don't really think I need a list," Rene said so low Clay could barely hear her.

Clay didn't know why he was so annoyed that Rene was making a list. "Just don't put Trace's name on that thing."

"I'm not going to put anyone's name on it," Rene said as she sat up straighter. "And you're the one who doesn't think people should just fall in love. I'd think you would *like* a list."

Clay had to admit she had a point. He should be in favor of a list like that; it eliminated feelings. It must be all this stress that was making him short-tempered. "If you're going to have a list, you may as well make the guy rich."

That should show he was able to join into the spirit of the thing.

"There's no need to ridicule—" Rene began.

"A good job does help," Mandy interrupted solemnly. "Especially when you start having babies. I'm hoping the job in Idaho pays well. We need a lot of things to set up our home."

"You should make a list of what you need for your house," Clay said encouragingly. Maybe the women would talk about clocks and chairs instead of husbands. He'd seen enough of life to know there were no fairy tale endings. Not in his life.

* * * * *

*Will spirited Rene Mitchell change trucker
Clay Preston's mind about love?
Find out in
SMALL-TOWN BRIDES,
the heartwarming anthology from
beloved authors
Janet Tronstad and Debra Clopton.
Available in June 2009
from Love Inspired®.*

Love Inspired®
SUSPENSE
RIVETING INSPIRATIONAL ROMANCE

These contemporary tales
of intrigue and romance
feature Christian characters
facing challenges to their faith...
and their lives!

**Four new Love Inspired Suspense titles are
available every month wherever books are
sold, including most bookstores, supermarkets,
drug stores and discount stores.**

Steeple
Hill®

Visit:
www.steeplehillbooks.com